J HENDERSON
Henderson, Jason,
The Triumph of Death /

ALEX
VAN HELSING

THE TRIUMPH
OF DEATH

Also by Jason Henderson

Alex Van Helsing: Vampire Rising
Alex Van Helsing: Voice of the Undead

ALEX VAN HELSING

THE TRIUMPH OF DEATH

JASON HENDERSON

HARPER TEEN

An Imprint of HarperCollinsPublishers

HarperTeen is an imprint of HarperCollins Publishers.

The Triumph of Death
Copyright © 2012 by Jason Henderson
www.epicreads.com

Library of Congress Cataloging-in-Publication Data is available.
ISBN 978-0-06-195103-9

Typography by Joel Tippie
12 13 14 15 16 LP/RRDH 10 9 8 7 6 5 4 3 2 1
❖
First Edition

For In Churl Yo, my friend

CHAPTER 1

Alex Van Helsing leapt from the plane without another thought, and in the corner of his eye he saw the black shape of the aircraft zip away, leaving him to plummet to earth or find a better option. As the ground roared toward him, Alex scanned the sky for vampires.

This was not how the end of the weekend was supposed to go. He should be doing flash cards right now. He should be trying to recognize the obscure names of monsters rather than diving after them.

"What is a stikini?" the computer voice had asked on the monitor earlier that evening. The word floated in silver on the screen, and Alex sat forward in the window seat, staring at the letters and searching his brain.

Beside him in the aisle seat, a broadly built Swedish agent named Hansen crossed his arms and threw a glance to see if maybe Alex had the answer. There was no one else who might know it; they were the last two agents on the flight.

Hansen and Alex were flying back from Anzio, Italy, where Alex and several other agents of the Polidorium— a secret organization funded by the black budgets of more than a dozen nations—had been studying at what everyone called Creature School. The school's actual name was P6 Identification Readiness Training, or PIRT, but Alex had tried using that acronym once and everyone had laughed at him. The purpose of Creature School was to familiarize the agents with the entities they might meet in the field. There were vampires out there, but those intelligent, dangerous beings were extremely varied, and Alex was only familiar with the most common kind. And of course there were plenty of other things to worry about.

Like everything else about Alex's time in the Polidorium, Creature School felt like a dream. His mentor in the Polidorium, Agent Sangster, had come to Alex just a few days before with news that he had pulled a few strings and gotten Alex a spot.

Alex's parents had given Sangster permission to create

excuses for getting Alex out of classes at his boarding school whenever it made sense—as long as Alex kept up his grades. This time the cover story was a soup kitchen dedication ceremony in a poor village in Romania, where Alex would supposedly be representing his own family's Van Helsing Foundation.

With time off from school procured, Alex flew out on a Friday morning from a military strip near Geneva, Switzerland, not far from his school, and by that afternoon he was walking through a secret lab hidden in the cliffs of the Italian shore.

Sangster himself hadn't come—the agent was also Alex's literature teacher and still had classes to teach. Besides, Sangster had already been through the training, so it was a rare opportunity for Alex to work alongside the Polidorium without his mentor looking over his shoulder.

They had started in a hospital-like building with long rows of glass cases and canisters where specimens floated inside. Alex and twelve other students walked behind a bald, slightly built teacher in a lab coat named Dr. Stu DeKamp, and every now and then DeKamp would stop and point out a specimen.

"This is a Caribbean jumbie skin." DeKamp pointed to a long, leathery thing with braided hair at the top.

"The jumbie is a vampire that can leave its skin behind while it travels on the air at night. Capture the skin and the creature will not survive long." Nods all around. "This is a chonchon, a Chilean flying head." The chonchon looked like a normal head with incongruous bat wings growing out of the sides of it. Alex had to stifle a mild laugh.

DeKamp had looked back to where Alex had been walking next to an agent in his twenties who had joined the Polidorium straight out of a police academy in Iowa. "Something you'd like to share?" DeKamp asked.

"Uh, no," Alex answered. "It's just that I have a friend who would absolutely kill to be seeing this." That would be Sid, a classmate of Alex's who seemed to know everything about vampires. Alex turned to Sid whenever he had a question about anything even remotely vampire-related, and he suspected that Sid would know what a chonchon was and would die to get a look at one.

"A friend at school?" asked the professor. Alex felt his face flush. This group of agents was young, but at fourteen, Alex was the prodigy. Everyone else was doing this as part of his or her job; Alex was still in high school. He shouldn't have laughed. He'd work on that. "Just be sure *you* learn it, Agent Van Helsing."

They saw more that afternoon: a vampiric pumpkin

that was actually still alive and tried to attack Alex through the cage, squashing its orange gourd self against the glass, a mouth opening red and mushing as it yearned for his blood. Alex's brain buzzed with a familiar, humming static, the awareness that something evil and dangerous was near.

They saw a pihuechenyi, a Central American winged snake that had been captured after it crashed into an airliner in the 1980s, dead and suspended from the ceiling.

Then, running around in a closed-off grassy area, they saw a sort of yellow-skinned, vein-covered centaur. It was a Scottish vampire called the nuckelavee and it had killed people all over a small group of islands called the Orkneys.

Dr. DeKamp called a break as they reached a commissary and stewards passed out bottled water. As Alex got his water he held up his hand. "I don't get it. Are these creatures vampires?"

"Well, it depends what the meaning of the word *vampire* is." DeKamp's holographic ID badge shimmered in the light, and Alex saw that the instructor was from Canada. The Polidorium was diverse, but a lot of the people Alex had met were from the United States, Britain, and Canada. Alex's friend Sid, also Canadian, would be thrilled to know that the resident creature genius among the Polidorium was one of his countrymen.

"*Vampire*," DeKamp continued, "is a word that does a lot of duty. Chiefly it refers to modified post-initial-failure humans; those creatures are generally the smartest ones, the ones calling the shots on the other side. But we can group into the realm of vampires anything that lives off the energy, blood, or flesh of others as long as it's touched by the curse."

"The curse?" Alex repeated.

"Any lion or snake, for example, lives off the flesh of others," explained DeKamp, "but they're not vampires. What distinguishes a vampire is that it carries what Polidori called the existential seed of corruption. The curse that turns men and creatures against their own souls."

Alex scrunched his face and DeKamp asked, "You're uncomfortable with the word *curse*?"

"Well, it just seems strange to hear a word so . . . magical."

DeKamp set down the bottle of water and came close. "You're the one who killed an augmented dog down in the Scholomance, right? And even you find the discussion of magic uncomfortable. Now think of the rest of the world. That is why our work must remain as secret as we can make it."

DeKamp turned. "*Talia sunt*, ladies and gentlemen." He beckoned them to continue the tour. "There are such things."

Two days later, Alex found himself actually accepted by the agents. They all suffered together through lectures on human vampires and their many variations—zombies, werewolves, and such—plus the myriad others broken into various parts of the plant and animal kingdoms. DeKamp also told them they all should take the training on vampire organizations, politics, and clans. Oh, and apparently witchcraft would take years.

This was a *great* weekend, and not a single thing that wasn't already behind glass actually tried to bite him, which was a nice change for an Alex/Polidorium activity.

And then on the plane ride home it all came crashing down.

The cabin of the Polidorium C-130 in which Alex and six of his fellow agents began the flight home did not have the battered metal interior that Alex had seen in the movies, with long benches and no frills. The plane was dressed up for comfort, with TVs on shiny gray walls; big, padded seats; and thick gray carpet bearing the stitched-in Polidorium crest and the words *Talia sunt*. Like DeKamp had said, this motto meant, "There are such things." It was an answer to a question, an answer to a doubt. *Don't tell yourself there are no such things. Of course there are, and we keep track of them.*

Agent Hansen and Alex sat together in front of a middle wall, or bulkhead, so they could take the PIRT creature quiz on a Polidorium computer mounted on the wall. When they left Anzio there had been five more agents spread out across the plane, but they had departed in Venice. It was eleven forty-five P.M.; with the layover, Alex had been traveling for about six hours.

"I know this one." Gunnar Hansen sat forward, wagging his finger. He had slightly curly, receding blond hair and a pug nose, and cheeks that were perpetually flushed. Alex always had the impression that Hansen was a Viking that someone had captured and shaved.

"Stikini." Alex repeated the word, watching the silver letters rotate on the screen. A thirty-second clock had begun to count down. Stikini. "It sounds like pasta."

"You're just hungry." Hansen gestured toward a go package, a Polidorium backpack usually filled with all manner of lethal and not-so-lethal stuff, which hung on a peg across from them, next to an emergency exit. "I have some granola bars."

"Wasn't there a steward?" Alex asked, looking up.

Hansen nodded. "That's right; where is he?"

Alex looked over the back of the seat toward the rear of the plane. "No one in the galley."

His neck was bugging him—Alex tugged at a collared shirt he had been wearing since Friday morning, a flexible polyvinyl "turtleneck" that was slightly bulky, threaded with strands of silver, and etched with crosses. They wore them all weekend at Creature School in case one of the captured creatures broke out. He'd need scissors to cut it off and hadn't gotten around to it. A vampire, meanwhile, could probably tear it loose if sufficiently motivated. So Alex was uncomfortable.

And hungry. When he was twelve, on a dare from his father, Alex had survived three days on only what he could catch or pick near their farm in Oklahoma, one of a handful of estates his family had in the United States. This was in January, when the trees were frozen black and snow blanketed the ground. And he had done fine. But now it seemed like every three hours his stomach grumbled, making him distracted and angry.

Stikini, the silver circling word continued. Five seconds. Then they would see the answer and lose points.

As if hearing Alex's mental howls, the cockpit door opened and a tall, wiry man with wisps of light brown hair and glasses emerged with an empty tray. When Alex saw the steward's glasses, his own eyes itched; he was longing to take out his contacts.

"There he is," said Hansen. The steward shut the cockpit door and glanced at them, heading toward the galley, presumably to get some food.

An image lit up in Alex's brain, a vampire image that faded into view. "Choctaw." Alex spoke to the computer. "Stikini is a Choctaw vampire that usually disguises itself as an owl."

As soon as the keywords Alex spoke registered with the computer, the countdown stopped and a diagram of the owl-vampire appeared.

"Not bad," Hansen said. "But it looks to me like an owl."

"It's an evil vampire owl." Alex smiled. But there was something wrong.

When Alex had thought of the owl, it had come to him in a rush, as if a part of his brain had opened up and growled at him. Alex looked back at the steward, who was bent over pulling plastic-wrapped sandwiches out of a cooler in the galley. He got nothing off the steward.

Alex rose from his seat and brushed past Hansen, stepping into the aisle. "Excuse me."

"Want me to pause it?" Hansen asked.

Standing in the aisle next to the emergency exit, Alex didn't answer. Maybe he was crazy, but he touched the wide gray cockpit door and felt the thin plastic bend slightly under his fingertips. If he understood the *static* in his brain at all—and really, he could not claim to understand it much—he could surely sense something evil through a plastic door.

He felt nothing.

Alex turned back and shrugged at Hansen as he reached the bulkhead seats.

"You okay?" Hansen asked, looking only a little concerned.

"Fine. Sorry. I think the steward is getting sandwiches."

As Alex sat, Hansen got up and reached for his go package. "You know, I want a granola bar anyway."

"Get me one, too." Alex turned back to the screen. "Let's see the next vamp—"

The cockpit door suddenly burst open and fell into shards.

A blurred, dark image ripped through the air, tearing into Hansen as it collided with him, sending the huge agent spinning end over end down the cabin. Alex saw Hansen's legs hit a set of seats in the back and the man cartwheeled with his own weight, finally crashing into the rear bulkhead.

The blur in the cabin slowed and became what Alex already knew it was—a vampire, though not one that Alex had met. The vampire's muscles strained against the borrowed Polidorium pilot's uniform he wore, and Alex saw dingy gray hair under the vampire's pilot cap as he whipped his head up and down the cabin, surveying his opponents.

Alex looked back at the cockpit and saw the mistake he'd made. The bent pieces of the door still stuck in its frame were about two inches thick and made of steel, with a thin plastic layer on top. When the door had opened once before, he had felt something briefly, some whiff of evil flowing from the cockpit. But otherwise the door was too thick to sense anything through, even when he touched it.

Alex could see another vampire, human-looking except for the alabaster skin and eyes that seemed to sparkle black, still sitting inside the cockpit at the controls of the plane.

"Get it under control!" came a roar from the cockpit.

Adrenaline rushed through Alex's body, tingling in his fingers, and he felt the edge of panic. He was on a plane with vampires, and—and then the questions began.

The tingling in your chest is a temptation to lose control. Don't listen to it. Ask the questions. What's going on?

The pilot vampire now emerged from the cockpit and ran to the back, and Alex heard a scream as the steward, who was already stammering into a radio, suddenly went quiet.

Vampires, Alex thought.

What do you have?

Alex looked at Hansen's go package, hanging where the agent had left it. For a moment he stole a glance back at the crumpled form of Hansen. In the go package, there would be all kinds of small weapons—a stake or two, some glass holy water grenades, and probably a gun. The gun would be useless on the plane, thought Alex, and anyway he had never used one. His own package—in the overhead compartment—never had a gun. But it would have something else good for close quarters, and he hoped Hansen's package would as well.

Alex jumped for the go package and grabbed it, crouching against the bulkhead. In an instant he was scrounging through the bag and found what he was looking for—an eighteen-inch, narrow, crossbow-like weapon, completely encased in heavy composite plastic and loaded with a cartridge of silver-threaded hawthorn wood bolts. A Polibow.

Alex heard a gasp farther back, in the galley, and looked beyond Hansen's body. The vampire dressed as the pilot had not killed the steward after all—he was hauling him forward, his arm wrapped around the steward's neck and shoulders.

"You!" the vampire in the pilot uniform called, pointing at Alex. The steward came under his own power, his legs moving rapidly to keep up with the muscular vampire.

Alex didn't waste any time with the Polibow. He reached in and grabbed a glass grenade, feeling the slosh of holy water inside, and threw it. The glass ball landed perfectly, with a heavy crunch, smacking the vampire on the head. It knocked his cap off as water flew in tinkles of glass, making the vampire's flesh sizzle. The vampire bared his teeth, but he didn't drop the steward.

"No, no." The vampire shook his head. His hair was sizzling, his flesh seeming to boil for a moment. He stuck a claw to the steward's neck, a long thumbnail digging in just below the crook of the thin man's jaw. The steward's eyes widened with terror behind his glasses. "We regret that there has been some turbulence, but if you'll just comply with the requests of the flight personnel you should soon be on your way." The pilot had an accent. Central American, Alex guessed, so that all his *you*s and *your*s came out *ju* and *jorr.*

Alex's static was roaring in his mind, and he realized the other vampire in the cockpit could be on him in a second, so he slammed back against the wall, his hand on the go package. He could reach for the Polibow. Could he hit the vampire and not the steward? Would the bolt hit faster than the vampire could move out of the way, or tear out the steward's throat?

"What do you want?" Alex asked.

"That's the spirit," the vampire said, flicking his head toward the computer in the bulkhead. "I need you to remove that tablet computer."

Alex moved a few inches along the wall until he was across from his seat and the bulkhead, so he could see the screen. It was still displaying the spinning image of the stikini.

The computer was a Polidorium tablet set into a wall cradle; it would pop in and out as needed. Except that Alex had no idea how to pop the tablet out.

"It's a terminal, a practice computer. It doesn't have anything on it," Alex said.

"Are you planning on just making things up or are you going to remove it for me?" the vampire growled, drawing a speck of blood from the steward's neck.

Alex had no idea what was on the computer. As far as

he was concerned it contained nothing but the training program. But it didn't matter now anyway.

"Okay." He edged toward the computer and stared at it.

"Hurry!" hissed the vampire.

"Okay!"

Alex studied the screen, which was embedded in a plastic frame in the bulkhead. He saw no obvious levers or buttons for dislodging it. "I may need a knife."

"You will *not* need a knife, I know that much," the vampire answered.

"If you know so much, why don't you get it?"

"Please!" the steward cried.

"Okay," Alex snapped. He tapped at the upper-left-hand corner of the screen. The words END SESSION? appeared. YES NO.

Yes.

"Ticktock!"

The steward howled again as the vampire dragged him forward so that Alex could see the thin trickle of blood trailing down his neck.

Alex turned back to the screen. The smell of bananas suddenly came to his nose, drifting strangely in and away. A bizarre, momentary olfactory hallucination. Stress and hunger. Alex shook his head to refocus.

A menu system appeared before him below the Poli-dorium logo.

He saw a button. *EJECT DEVICE.*

Alex tapped the button and the device popped for-ward and out, the ten-inch Plexiglas tablet going dark as it came away from its cradle in the wall. He caught it and stood, turning to the vampire and the steward.

The steward looked glassy-eyed and afraid.

The banana smell came to Alex again.

"Give it here!" the vampire demanded, holding out his free hand. "Bjurman! We can go!"

The second vampire emerged instantly from the cockpit.

Alex felt his eyes tracking the trickle of the steward's blood. It was blackish and strange, and the smell of bananas was stronger.

Alex still held the device and looked at the steward. "So where are you from?"

"Please . . ."

They were wearing pilots' uniforms. Alex had seen the pilots when he'd boarded, and though he hadn't got-ten a good look at them, they hadn't been vampires then. So they had stolen the uniforms and taken the pilots' places during the layover. But they needed someone to hold hostage aboard a plane of agents. Even a steward couldn't be trusted to be compliant.

"What's your name?" Alex asked the steward.

"Give me the device!" ordered the pilot.

"I . . . ," said the steward.

Bananas. That meant something. Then he thought, *Filipino.* A Filipino illusion, and a very unusual one.

"What's two plus two?"

"Please . . ."

"You can't *do* math, can you? Just a couple lines of dialogue, that's all you can handle." Alex drew the Polibow from his belt and pointed it at all of them, backing toward the bulkhead. "Get back in the cockpit and fly the plane."

"Hand it over," said the vampire, "or this man dies."

"I don't think so." Alex fired the Polibow.

The Aswang vampires of the Philippines could replace people with simple doppelgangers. These doppelgangers were zombie-like in nature and didn't last long.

And they were made of banana leaves.

Of course an Aswang didn't *look* like banana leaves—the glamour that transformed them smoothed over the vegetable matter and gave them the appearance of normal, if sallow, human beings. But there was no disguising the smell and the beginnings of rot.

The bolt struck the steward in the chest and the steward's eyes burst like banana-filled tomatoes, his body disintegrating into leaves and sweet-smelling mush. Alex fired at the pilot vampire as the steward fell apart, but the vampire pushed the falling mass toward Alex. Alex missed.

The copilot yanked on the emergency exit—something Alex wasn't expecting—and suddenly wind and papers and the last vestiges of the banana leaf man were flying out the door. Alex drew his Polibow again and the vampire smacked him across the face, sending him flying back.

Alex could now barely hear over the roar of wind. He watched Gunnar Hansen's body lift with the sudden bucking of the plane and smash to the floor.

Alex felt the plane begin to pitch slightly and then steady, fighting to stay on course. Obviously the autopilot was functioning, or else the plane would surely be diving toward the earth. But as the plane jolted, the tablet computer slipped from his hand, bouncing off the bulkhead near the vampire. About thirty oxygen masks dropped from the ceiling.

As Alex steadied himself against a seat, he saw the pilot had already picked up the computer and attached it to a cord that ran to an iPod-like device on his belt. The pilot vampire studied the connection between the two devices for a second, watching a few lights blinking on his own device. Then, as the blinking slowed, he nodded and tossed the Polidorium tablet aside. "Okay."

The copilot nodded in agreement, removing his jacket to reveal a parachute attached to his shoulders. He snapped the clasps across his chest and disappeared through the door without another signal.

"*Gracias, amigo!*" called the pilot, and he bounded past Alex in a blur. The vampire stopped at the door, looking back. "I've heard you are always prepared. I'll bet you weren't prepared for this!" With that, the vampire leapt out the door.

Alex ran after the vampire and stopped, holding on. He paused for a moment and stared across the entire plane.

Just him and the late Hansen, who absolutely had not expected his last act to be that of searching for a granola bar.

Could he fly the plane?

You can't fly a plane.

And then something in the cockpit burst with orange and red, and Alex saw flames rising with the smell of burning plastic and black smoke.

Okay. Okay, now you're in trouble.

Chest flooding. That's panic. Ask the questions.

In microseconds, questions shot across Alex's mind like ricocheting bullets.

What's going on?

I'm alone at 30,000 feet. The cockpit has been destroyed. The door is open.

What do you need to get down?

A parachute.

Do you have one?

No.

Is there one nearby?

Alex saw a small door clasped shut near the cockpit. He tore it open, hoping to find a parachute. No such luck.

Who has one?

No time. The smell of smoke was getting thicker. He looked around for something to protect his eyes from the wind and saw his motorcycle helmet rolling against the bulkhead. He slapped it on his head and slipped his arms through the straps of the go package. He was out of time.

He drew near to the door, looked out, took a deep breath, and leapt.

Alex flipped once in the wind, totally losing control. For a moment he was thankful that he could barely see the ground—just a distant line of tiny lights dotting the landscape like LEDs on a model train set. He could see a train, in fact, far below, a long stream of bright yellow lights pulsing out of the sides of the cars.

He spotted the first vampire farther below, finally, his parachute shimmering in the darkness, barely visible—a brilliant red vinyl canopy.

This is crazy. You're going to die shot through his head and he shut it down. *Breathe. This is your only chance.*

He was falling. Without a parachute. He scanned the air some more, *Find it find it,* and spotted the second vampire. Both seemed about a quarter mile or more away, not far from one another. *I pick that one.* Alex tilted forward, bringing his arms close to his sides, and began to dive.

The wind smashed against his Plexiglas wind visor and roared, rolling the skin of his face back toward his ears. The vampire he'd chosen seemed to be banking a little, slower than the other, and Alex aimed for him.

Within a hundred yards Alex began to worry. If he struck the parachute he would wrap himself up and fall to the earth in a cloth cocoon. If he struck the vampire's body with his head, he was pretty sure his neck would break.

He thought about flipping again and striking the

vampire with his feet, but for a grisly millisecond he pictured hitting the vampire with such force, all located in his heels, that he would sail clear through the creature's body and plummet toward the earth, torn to shreds by its jagged ribs as he passed through.

Hug the vampire, body to body. That had to be the way.

Alex had the vampire's body in sight and prepared to strike. When he could see his face and shining eyes, Alex extended his arms wide, as if he were about to hug a tree.

The vampire looked up in shock just as Alex came rolling in at full speed. Suddenly Alex's vision went out completely. Static roared in his brain like a lion, and for a moment it was as though he could see systems clicking on, sparks of electricity in his blacked-out vision kicking him awake once more. Alex heard the parachute lurch loudly as the vampire grunted.

His vision returned and he found himself hugging the vampire chest to chest. He grabbed on to the straps, and they began to spin.

The vampire moved quickly from shocked to confused to enraged. *"Dudo! Idiot!"* he heard the vampire cry as they spun, the parachute tilting this way and that as they swung. The vampire reared back his head and then lunged his teeth for Alex. He felt the press of fangs against the turtleneck and heard the sizzle of flesh and saliva against the silver lining. The pressure smarted, though, and Alex angrily butted the vampire in the head with his helmet. "Stop that!"

"This is my parachute!" the vampire yelled, though Alex could barely hear him over the sound of the wind and through the plastic visor. There was something insane and almost merry in his sparkling eyes.

"I'm joining you, and we can fight when we hit the ground!" Alex yelled.

"No," the vampire shouted. "It's too much weight! Which one of us do you think will survive hitting the ground, eh?"

Alex looked down to see a grassy field, barely visible in the moonlight. Even with the parachute, the ground was coming up fast. He understood now. The parachute had been prepared for just the vampire, who probably weighed less than Alex did, even with his muscular frame. Vampires were cat-like, fast and light.

The vampire tried to kick him away, and Alex held on, smashing him in the nose briefly before yanking back from the teeth once more.

They were hurtling toward the ground now. He judged he had another hundred yards to go. Alex loosed one of his hands and reached back to his go package.

"So we die together, no?" The vampire had an insane look in his eye.

"Nope," Alex yelled.

"What makes you so sure?"

"I have something that *you* don't have," Alex answered, "and it's going to give me some more time."

"What's that?"

Alex brought the Polibow to the vampire's chest and pulled the trigger, feeling a solid *thump* as the bolt slammed between the creature's ribs and into his heart.

"Hot air."

The vampire roared and Alex dropped his Polibow and wrapped his elbows around the straps. He yanked up and away as far as possible, pressing his face against his forearms as a fireball erupted where the creature had been.

Alex saw the orange flash burst against his wind visor and cringed as the helmet heated up immediately. As he closed his eyes the flash blazed brilliantly for a split second. The wave of fire and hot air pushed in all directions, and Alex was yanked sharply upward as the parachute caught the air and rose a full twenty yards.

Alex opened his eyes and yelped; his leather jacket was on fire, and he started patting it down wildly with his free hand as he spun. For a moment he worried the parachute would catch fire, but like a hot air balloon, it merely expanded and rose with the sudden burst from the vampire.

Alex spun with the straps, hanging on for dear life, his legs churning wildly.

The parachute whipped and lurched as the earth came toward him once more, and Alex hit the soft grass running. Even so, he felt the shock in his knees and ran through it, releasing the straps and tottering forward, flipping end over end until he finally rolled to a stop, singed and bruised but alive.

Near the horizon, a second fireball erupted with a distant *boom* as the plane slammed to the ground, lighting up the clouds with orange and yellow.

Alex sat for a moment and caught his breath. He then fished a cell phone out of his pocket and punched in some numbers. Within half an hour, the air filled with the sound of rotor blades.

CHAPTER 2

Six hours later, he was back at Glenarvon-LaLaurie School on the banks of Lake Geneva as though nothing unusual had occurred.

"You've got to tell me everything," Sid Chamberlain, Alex's ginger-haired Canadian roommate, said as he walked with Alex to the cafeteria. Alex still felt a twinge of pain in his knees, but all told, the worst he had to deal with were some mild burns on his forearms. Paul Messina, his other roommate, was walking ahead of them, so broad of shoulder that he acted as a human icebreaker, spreading the traffic of students in the halls out around them.

Alex picked up a nervous sort of buzz in the air, most

of it about upcoming travel. As he sped through the busy halls of the school in the morning, his stomach raging with hunger, he could hear people exchanging plans. Two weeks to the fall break, Alex still had not decided if he would be going home.

"I think they just wanted the computer." Alex answered when Sid asked why the attack on the plane had happened.

"So what about this *creature school*?" Sid's eyes were on fire with the idea of a deep study of the races of vampires. When he wasn't working on his own fiction, Sid spent every remaining waking minute studying vampires for Scarlet World, a game that he liked to play. Sid had stacks of characters he had designed based on the reference books he kept.

"Oh, that." They were turning into the cafeteria now, and Paul led them straight to a table in the back right corner. *There she was.* Minhi Krishnaswami was wearing a sweater jacket and waving to them.

Minhi gave Paul a chaste peck as they took a seat in a clatter of chairs and dropped backpacks. "You're back!" Minhi called, and Alex wanted to hug her, but he was already engaged in sitting down and had blown the chance. Wasn't right to want to anyway. She was Paul's girlfriend and there was nothing else to say.

Minhi placed her palms flat on the table and leaned forward, eyes crinkling with her smile. "So?"

Alex said to everyone, "Did you know that there's a vampire that's just a head, but it has bat wings coming out of its ears?"

"Yeah, that's the chonchon." Sid nodded. "Did you see one?"

"A dead one."

"Oh my *God*," Sid practically panted.

Paul chuckled. "Yes, yes, oh my God. *Did you know*," he repeated in his London accent, slapping the table and looking at Minhi, "that our man in Switzerland threw himself out of a bloody *plane* last night?"

Minhi's mouth formed a confused O. "What?"

"In my defense, that was really the strongest option on the table." Alex looked around. "I'm starving."

"Here, here," Paul said, and they stood and headed to the front of the cafeteria. They dropped all talk of planes and bat wings for the duration. These were Alex's . . . what were they? Confidants? Friends, but friends that knew his secrets.

Alex had a lot of secrets to keep, but to be fair he'd been playing fast and loose with all of them. In the past three months since he had come to Glenarvon Academy, which had since merged with their sister school,

LaLaurie, Alex had learned to walk a daily tightrope that relied very much on the completely unsupervised discretion of the circle of friends he had entrusted with the details of his second and more unusual life. These three, Paul and Sid and Minhi, knew how much time Alex spent training with the agents of the Polidorium and they took it in stride, as Paul explained it, the way they might accommodate an Olympic speed skater with a demanding coach.

A discreet part of Alex wondered if he had made some mistake sharing so much with them, but he couldn't have it any other way. He would have liked to have been a loner and kept it all to himself, but he needed the feeling of acceptance and normalcy they brought. He tried not to think of the danger their closeness might invite. Whenever he went down that path in his mind he stopped himself, defiantly refusing to consider it. It was a massive, deliberate hole in his calculations, one he both knew about and could not bear to think about. They kept his secrets and he hoped that he would not get them killed.

At the cafeteria line, Alex doubled up on eggs, toast, and fruit. He thought he was surely eating as much as Paul, who was a full head taller, but discovered on inspection that this was not the case.

"How did you get home?" Minhi whispered as she stood beside him and they slowly moved sideways along the cafeteria line. "Did you get any sleep?"

"Uh, I had a cell in my backpack and called my 'friends.' And as for sleep—" He shrugged. "Eh."

"You can't manage on no sleep." Minhi clucked. "Even you." *Say more things,* he wanted to say. Her accent, with its slight Indian lilt, was endlessly wonderful to listen to.

"I'll be sure to bring that up at the next meeting," Alex whispered. The next meeting, in fact, would be at noon, where he would see his handlers—including Sangster, his mentor—for another debriefing. They had conducted a preliminary one during the helicopter ride early in the morning. Truthfully he was used to very little sleep, and anyway, with luck he could catch up on the weekend. Which was five days away and counting.

Trays in hand, they all turned back and headed for their table again. Alex watched as a couple of girls waved at Sid. "Do we get Part Three?" one asked.

Sid nodded. "Friday." The girls rushed off and Sid shrugged back at Alex.

"Part Three?" Alex repeated.

"'The Owner of Pier Fifty-seven,'" Sid said. "It's a three-part story for the lit club. It's my turn to read this Friday."

"Have you written it yet?" Paul asked. Sid shrugged again, which probably meant no. In the short time Alex had known him, Sid had progressed from being terrified at the thought of any public performance to becoming a minor celebrity for the short stories that he was reading aloud and also publishing in the weekly school paper. Alex had no idea where Sid found the time to fit them into his class work.

As they drew near their table, Alex's attention snapped to a girl standing in the cafeteria entrance. The first thing that caught his eye was the strange chaos of her black hair, a boiling storm of oddly placed pigtails and ponytails, her skin white and eyes so light blue they were almost clear. She was standing with her hands in front of her, fingers curled into one another as though she were about to sing, and her pointed chin and slightly nervous look reminded him of a curious bird. She wore long blue tights and a weird blue minidress with wide puffed shoulders that made the whole outfit seem less like a dress than a strange suit of armor.

They reached the table and Alex put down his tray. As he looked back, the girl's glance swept the room again and then caught his eyes almost accidentally.

Alex's mouth was hanging open with the unsaid question, *Who . . . ?*

Paul followed his eyes. "*She's* new."

Minhi was popping a grape into her mouth and said, covering her lips, "Yes she is." She swallowed and waved as the girl looked back her way, this time registering recognition, her wide smile going all the way to her eyes. "Astrid!"

The new girl was already moving swiftly to the table. She seemed to bounce with her steps and greeted Minhi as though they were old friends, with a kiss on the cheek. Paul rose and silently reminded Alex and Sid that they should, too.

"I hope I'm not intruding." Astrid's voice was full and musical, low in her throat, and Alex detected a hint of an accent. Dutch? "Guys, this is Astrid Gretelian," Minhi said. "She just came to the girls' floor last night."

"You're starting in the middle of the year?" Alex asked before he even knew what he was going to say. He never could get introductions right.

This seemed to catch her by surprise. The girl's head swiveled back and her eyes gleamed with her smile, her whole body swaying. Then she dramatically nodded her head at him. "Yes, I hope that's allowed."

"I think we'll make an exception in your case." Paul extended a large hand. "Paul."

Minhi and Alex exchanged glances. Whatever charm

Paul had, it lacked an off switch.

Alex gave the new girl his own name and Sid waved. "Sid."

"We only allow him a few syllables a day," said Paul. They all sat.

"Aren't you going to eat?" Minhi asked the new girl.

Astrid shook her head. "I don't know if there's time; I'm supposed to go and meet with Ms. . . ."

"Daughtry?" Alex suggested. That was the girls' assistant headmistress. If her meeting was anything like the one Alex had on his first day, it would include an uncomfortably frank discussion of any past history and plans for success, or whatever term for not screwing up they would use. But then again, that had been Alex's experience with the boys' headmaster, Otranto. Maybe the girls had it easier.

"Yes, yes, exactly." Astrid looked at Alex. "Three sentences from you and two of them have ended in a question mark."

"Here, I have . . ." Minhi looked at the plate of fruit she'd brought to the table. "Do you want my banana?" Astrid took the banana graciously, opening it monkey-style, from the bottom rather than the stem. She nibbled at it, her bony shoulders moving with her jaw.

Minhi turned to the guys. "Astrid is from the

Netherlands. Her parents had to move to Switzerland for work."

"My mother's work. She's doing a lot of traveling right now, so this was the best fit." Astrid put her hand on Minhi's shoulder. "So apparently I'm Minhi's assignment."

Minhi shook her head. "Hardly. Anyone new needs a sister, so I'm showing her around until she gets settled."

"A buddy system." Alex understood that well enough. If Paul and Sid hadn't taken him under their wings when he'd come in he wouldn't have lasted two days. Almost didn't, as it turned out. "Is she your new roommate, too?" he asked. Minhi's last roommate, Vienna, had left abruptly about a month ago and wasn't expected back anytime soon. He was shocked to find he had not thought of her in a week or so.

"Nope," Minhi said. "I've still got my own room, thank God."

"Me too," Astrid said. "I opted for a single room. It's . . ."

"Tiny?" Minhi offered.

"I like to think of it as cozy." Astrid's smile emanated seismic waves of warmth. She turned to Paul. "So you're the boyfriend," she said, sizing him up.

Paul folded his arms. "Ohh, you've talked."

"And you are the writer." She looked at Sid.

"She told you that?" Sid smiled as he looked out from beneath the reddish curls that were growing longer recently.

"*She* did, plus about four other girls who tried to give me the entire *dramatis personae* before I went to sleep," Astrid explained. "You have fans."

"*Groupies*," Paul said, clapping Sid's shoulder.

"And you . . . are . . ." Astrid's eyes narrowed as she took a bite of the banana and swallowed. Finally she shrugged. "Alex."

"Just Alex." He repeated the word, echoing her shrug. "I'm working on an 'Alex the' but I'm not there yet." Alex wondered what kind of epithet his friends might have provided if they were alone. *Alex the guy who got us kidnapped? Alex the guy who stole a WaveRunner to get to the Charity Ball?* "Stick around and maybe you can suggest something."

"I'll be on the lookout." Astrid's English was so perfect that she must have begun speaking it as a child, possibly at home. He didn't detect any Britishisms. Maybe an American father? Alex pushed the thought away. He had to stop this, analyzing every newcomer as though they were a schematic on one of the Polidorium's displays.

"So here's how it will work," said Paul, drumming the table. "Minhi can help you through the social stuff because we're hopeless. But you won't be rid of us. Sid can tutor you in just about anything, and Alex and I will be available for color commentary."

"At least one of you is dead weight," Astrid observed wryly. "You can work in shifts."

Alex laughed. "Well, we won't keep you prisoner. You may actually make *other* friends. But if Minhi's got your back, we do, too."

The bell rang. "Oh!" Astrid looked alarmed, and her whole body carried the change in vibration. She stood. "I was supposed to . . ."

"Daughtry," Alex reminded her.

Astrid rose and kissed Minhi on the cheek once more. She bobbed like a bird ahead of them and turned briefly to Alex. "I'll keep an eye out."

"For what?"

"For whatever should come after 'Alex the,'" she said, smiling, before disappearing down the hall.

CHAPTER 3

At 11:55 on the dot, Alex's phone buzzed on the way out of his Algebra class, jolting his body to readiness just as he was feeling the doldrums of almost no sleep. He was fishing it out of his jacket as Minhi tugged at his sleeve.

BACK GATE, read the text. It was time to meet Sangster. He looked up at Minhi. "Hmm?"

"What are your plans this afternoon?" Minhi asked.

Paul and Sid had pulled up ahead, and Alex was about to call to them and ask. "I don't know, what are we doing?"

"Just . . ." Minhi looked ahead. "I wanted to ask you . . ."

Alex held up a hand as his phone buzzed again. *Okay,*

okay. He looked at her. "I'm sorry, what?"

Minhi shrugged. "We'll figure it out."

"Okay." Alex nodded. "Guys! I'll catch you later." He shot down the hall, leaving the three of them behind. For a moment he caught a glimpse of Astrid moving into the library. They apparently shared no classes; he hadn't seen her all morning.

As he passed the library, the cavernous, dark space yawned at him, with its ladders and catwalks and shadows. The girl had been swallowed up completely by it, as he reckoned anyone could be. He hit the side door and was outside, cold air snapping at his chin and ears.

The black Polidorium van that pulled up by the back gate barely slowed as the side door slid open. For a moment Alex's body tensed at the thought that it could be a decoy, a stolen van full of Scholomance vampires out to capture him—it wouldn't be the first time—but instantly he saw the extended hand of Mr. Sangster.

"Let's go, Alex." Sangster grabbed his hand and yanked him inside. By the time Alex had sat down across from his literature teacher, the van was moving and picking up speed, heading down the road to town.

Wearing chinos and a black sweater and jacket, the man who sat across from Alex was many things, and a teacher was only one of them. An expert in vampire

activity and a well-placed ground leader for the organization, Sangster had been Alex's entre into the Polidorium,
and had taken him under his wing the moment Alex
had arrived at Glenarvon Academy. When Alex got to
Switzerland, he had known nothing of the secret world
that the Polidorium inhabited. He had learned a lot of
things in a very short amount of time, including that his
own father had been preparing him all his life, without
his knowledge, to work with the Polidorium.

Dad had taught Alex how to survive on little sleep and
food, how to control the panic that hit people in tense
situations, how to fight and ski and (illegally) drive,
and even, if necessary, jump out of a plane. But Dad
had denied completely the existence of vampires and
never let on that soon Alex would be involved in fighting them. It had happened sooner than intended. Dad,
it turned out, had actually been an agent for the Polidorium. He had spent his life fighting vampires because it
was the calling of his family, the Van Helsings, who had
helped found the Polidorium in its early days. And then
Dad had met Mom and retired, and lied for all fourteen
years Alex and his sisters had been alive.

Only recently had Dad told Alex the truth and laid
the burden of deciding what to do next at his feet. "We're
part of a war," Dad had told him. It was a war with the

vampires on one side and the Polidorium and the dwindling numbers of the Van Helsing family on the other. "Whether you want to join it now is up to you."

"Are we going to the farmhouse?" Alex asked. Sangster was flipping through a manila folder as the van rocked, and Alex clicked a safety belt over his shoulder.

"There's been a change of plans." Sangster looked back at the driver and passenger seat in front. He gestured. "Armstrong?"

Alex didn't know the driver, but he saw Anne Armstrong, a woman with short blond hair and freckles, climb out of the passenger seat, bobbing slightly as the van moved. She dropped into a seat next to Sangster.

"We read your debrief from this morning," Armstrong said in her usual business-like American accent. "You're sure they left the computer on the plane?"

Alex nodded. "The computer they dropped, yeah." The van swerved around a corner and Alex was momentarily blinded by a streak of sunlight that glinted through the windows. "But the vampire had a connection of some sort—"

"A dongle?" Armstrong asked.

"Yeah, he clicked it in and I would think he downloaded everything on there. But I don't get it; wasn't that just a training device?"

Sangster shook his head. "It should have been. It should have been a tablet that was practically empty except for run-of-the-mill low-security info."

"Yeah, I don't think the Scholomance needs to know how many different kinds of vampires there are on the planet. Maybe they want to know what we know."

"First," said Sangster, "they probably have a decent feel for that. And second, this was a fairly complicated op considering they could have stolen one of those training tablets from any number of places, including half a dozen vans scooting around Europe."

"Was it a terminal? Maybe hooked into the Polidorium network?" Alex asked.

"Absolutely," Armstrong said, catching the implication. The vampires could have used the computer to introduce a virus into the system, one the Polidorium had not been alerted to yet.

Alex shrugged, opening his hands. "Sooo . . ."

"So all this is fascinating, but we already know that they were acting on big plans," Sangster said.

Alex pursed his lips. "Well, maybe. How do you know?"

Sangster looked over his shoulder as they made another turn, and Alex gasped. Up ahead, the sunlight struck the concrete of the road and made shadows in the trees, and then the road and the scenery around it all . . . ended. At once.

They were rolling toward a suspended wall of blackness, a liquid barrier that rippled over the road.

"What *is* that?" Alex asked.

"That is the town of Secheron," said Sangster. "And it is dark at noon."

CHAPTER 4

As though going through an invisible tunnel, the van pierced an inky curtain of darkness and entered nighttime on the other side. Alex felt a wave of instinctual revulsion course through his body. Within moments they rolled on to the long, cozy main street that carried traffic into the town square and beyond, and the streets were filling up with people. Alex tried to take in everyone, shopkeepers and shoppers milling about nervously, eyeing the sky and one another, a pair of men fighting on the sidewalk outside a bar. He saw someone about to throw a chair through a window. The village of Secheron, which Alex associated with tourists, bookshops, and bars on piers at the fairly swank marina, was going insane. It looked like—

"It's a war zone." Sangster pulled a black hard-sided suitcase out from under his seat. He undid the buckles, the metal clasps clacking loudly. Outside, police sirens blared and darts of red and yellow light flickered through the windows.

"Whoa!" Alex said, scanning the horizon and momentarily confused. "What are those? Buildings?"

Sangster looked out. In the distance, there appeared to be flickering fires coming from cities that were near total destruction. Sangster tapped the window. "Huh." He shook his head.

"What?" Alex asked.

"That's due west. You know what's there? Water. The lake. What you're seeing is an illusion." They appeared to be encircled by distant cities on fire. "And this illusion is surrounding us."

"Like one of those three-hundred-and-sixty-degree movies at Disney World," Alex said. "Amazing."

"In as much as it's big enough to encase this whole town, you bet it's amazing." Sangster sounded slightly alarmed.

"Driver, gimme the screen back here," Armstrong called, and after a moment one of the windows darkened and filled with an image in gray and green, with splotches of orange.

"What's that?" Alex asked. They passed a police car

parked at the side of the street where a Swiss policeman was getting out, running to one of the shops.

Armstrong put a wireless mobile piece in her ear and swiped a hand over the image. "This is the village, satellite photography. The orangeish images you see are people." She indicated the clusters of orange blobs on streets that Alex could identify by a faint blue map grid. "They're gathering in the streets and the square; I see a lot of them at the marina. I don't see any blues."

By *blues*, Armstrong was referring to the way vampires appeared on Polidorium infrared systems, which were enhanced to make especially cold creatures pop. You couldn't photograph vampires, but you could save an infrared image of them, and the Polidorium files were filled with pencil sketches and digital infrared shots. Alex had heard that the earliest attempts at field use of infrared had failed because the vampires simply blended in too much; the enhancements had been a major leap forward.

"There has to be." Sangster sounded confused. "Could they be camouflaged?"

"Not against us." Armstrong shook her head and took a heavy jacket that Sangster offered her, slipping it on over her blouse.

The van swerved as a man on an old motor scooter

swooped in front of them, barely missing them. The scooter didn't have its headlights on. It wobbled across the street and Alex winced as it sideswiped a curb next to a flower shop and toppled over. It wasn't a fatal fall.

"Blues? You think the Scholomance is behind—what exactly is this?"

"This is nothing we've ever seen before," Sangster said.

"When did it happen?" Alex asked.

"About forty-five minutes ago a cloud, heavy, like a storm cloud, started gathering over Secheron near the marina. Except that it kept growing and expanding." He gestured out the window. "It's not just blocking the sun from above—it's as though the whole town has been encased in nightfall. That perimeter we drove through is the edge of it."

"It's magical," Alex said. "Like the entrance to the Scholomance." The vampire organization was hidden behind various doors, which boasted similar permeable curtains. "Wait—how do you know we'll be able to drive back out now that we're in?"

"We don't know anything right now," Armstrong answered. "But we saw some cars speeding out of the city, so it doesn't look like it's that kind of seal."

Alex heard the crash of glass as one of the shop

windows disintegrated. He didn't see anything that had been thrown, but then he saw someone running out with a cash register.

"Are these people crazy? Are they under some kind of spell?"

Sangster jogged his head back and forth as if he were tossing the idea around. "We can't tell. What do you feel?"

"What?"

"What do you *feel*?" Sangster repeated the question, and Alex shrank back physically, feeling cornered. The strange skills he possessed were not something for which he had a rule book.

Alex opened his hands. "Why would I feel anything? I can sense vampires, but—"

"Can you sense any right now?"

"I don't know!"

"Think," Sangster ordered. "We know you can sense when they're near or when there's some sort of dark evil at work. What do you feel now?"

Alex shook his head. "Nothing specific." He wanted to come up with more, but he couldn't report what he didn't understand. "I was . . . when we got here I felt sick, a little. Is that helpful?"

"Maybe." Sangster tapped his own forehead. "We

gotta get this thing squared away if it's gonna be useful in the field, Alex."

"Yeah, I'm working on that." Alex looked at them both.

Sangster handed Armstrong an automatic weapon about the size of a briefcase.

"This looks like more than just darkness," Alex said, indicating the running crowds. "People don't instantly run through the streets and start attacking people because it's dark outside. So maybe it's something like a—"

"A gas, a nerve agent." Armstrong looked at Sangster. "Get masks."

Sangster pulled out three lightweight rubber masks and passed them around, and Alex copied the others as they put them over their heads. Like the agents, Alex let his lie on his forehead. He took off his school jacket and pulled on the one Sangster handed him, and felt heavy plates of composite plastic inside the lining thump against his chest. There was a patch on the shoulder that read TALIA SUNT.

"If it's magic, though, there's no guarantee these will stop it," Sangster said.

"If it's a magic fear-maker or whatever," Alex countered, "wouldn't we be feeling it already?"

Armstrong shook her head, pointing at the ceiling and walls of the van. "This van is a rolling fortress against that kind of thing. Silver lining in the body, hawthorn wood threaded throughout, holy water injected into a filament mesh layer. Plus a few favors we don't discuss. We are protected."

"So I guess just staying in the van isn't gonna happen."

Sangster handed him a go package to throw over his shoulders. Alex felt the whole thing over before putting it on, making sure the easy-access pockets were unsecured and filled. "Alex, we're the first to respond. There won't be any more agents for at least another fifteen minutes, so we need to be careful. I need you here, though. I'm hoping your skills will give us some kind of edge."

"My skills that we don't really know anything about."

"No time like the present."

They were moving through the Secheron town square now, a usually pleasant place where people were now running in every direction. Two men were fighting on top of an overturned metal café table. Alex heard more sirens and saw police vans pulling into the square. Police officers in full riot gear leapt instantly from the sides.

"I never knew Secheron had a SWAT team."

Sangster nodded. "I see four cops in gear and I'm betting that's all they have."

The van yanked left and was moving down a street Alex knew well, dotted with restaurants and bars and more shops, sloping downhill. "We're going to the marina?"

Sangster and Armstrong seemed to exchange silent messages. Alex watched as they both suddenly relaxed, their shoulders rolling down as they sat back in the seat.

Sangster slowly drew a breath. "Civil unrest is not our thing. Be ready, we're stopping in about one minute."

Armstrong looked up. "Blue."

Alex followed her eyes. There on the satellite image, a strange blue emanation was gathering and pulsing right at the edge of the water, among the piers of the marina.

The van screeched to a halt in the cobblestoned drive, and Alex took in the whole scene beyond—a long pier with a two-story restaurant at the end, two more nearly as large with one-story bars of their own, and countless jetties with small boats. All were encased in darkness. He checked his watch; the silver cross in the clasp glinted green as it reflected the satellite screen. It was twenty-five minutes past noon.

The engine idled as they watched people running down the piers. The restaurant at the end of one flickered now, and Alex saw smoke pouring out of its side. Then his eye caught something else.

"Look."

"I see it," Sangster responded. They pulled closer to the window to see water swirling around off the end of the main pier, kicking up a furious foam.

"So what's the plan?" It occurred to Alex that he hadn't asked. "What are we doing?"

"We're the first to see what's happening." Armstrong went to the door and prepared to pull it open. She tugged the mask down over her mouth, leaving the top half of her face exposed, and Alex and Sangster did the same. Alex pulled the Polibow out of the side of his go package and looked at it. It was a later model than he often used, with twice as many bolts in the magazine—meaning he had sixteen shots.

Sangster tapped the mobile piece in his ear and Alex heard the tap in his own. Then the teacher briskly nodded at Armstrong.

Armstrong yanked the door open and they hustled out, Alex forming up behind them at the back of the van.

At first there was only the sound of confused people ranging around the jetties and the wind clanking lines against sailboat masts. All three of them kept their eyes on the water.

The roiling whirlpool at the edge of the marina churned and spewed water, and they heard an almost electric series of cracks and pops that echoed like gunshots. Alex felt a wave of static in his head come hard and fast, roaring insistently. "Here it comes."

The surface seemed to rip open, and Alex saw a strange shape bursting up around the pier: A latticework of white rolled up out of the lake, like a great, grasping skeletal claw, and grabbed on to the pier. He saw silhouettes moving among the latticework, as if a band of people were climbing quickly up a flight of stairs.

And then the invasion began.

CHAPTER 5

"Everyone, get away!" Sangster waved his arms as they moved forward from the van, closing the distance to the long boardwalk that connected with the main pier. A man and woman running out of the restaurant nearly collided with him.

Armstrong spoke rapidly into her Bluetooth. "Farmhouse, this is Armstrong, Sangster, and Van Helsing. We are at the pier—we have an incursion of Scholomance vampires emerging from the water."

Alex heard another female voice, farther away, click on. "Acknowledged. Reinforcements are on the way."

"How many?" They reached the edge of the pier, watching a steadily approaching crowd of white-clad vampires with something strange about their faces, something Alex still couldn't make out.

"Four vans, just now entering Secheron by the main road. ETA five minutes."

"We're going to need more than that, and faster," Sangster cut in.

One of the vampires on the pier caught a woman in a blue coat, biting viciously at her throat. The woman went down and the vampire rose again, moving on.

The team hugged a wide telephone pole and Sangster watched the advancing horde tear into the crowd of townspeople. "They're not feeding, just attacking. We can't get a clean shot until these people are clear," he added in frustration.

The group was still a hundred yards off, and Alex nearly ran into another pedestrian. The look in the man's eyes was a confused sort of terror. "That way!" Alex shouted, waving him off.

Now Alex saw what was strange about the vampires' faces. The nearest one, the one who had attacked the woman in the blue coat, would normally have looked like a flash of white in the darkness, skin all alabaster save for sparkling eyes. But this one wore heavy black splotches of paint around his eyes and over his nose. He looked like a skeleton.

"They're painted like skeletons." Alex scanned the others he could see. "Why?"

"It's odd. I don't remember them painting that way." Sangster's voice on the radio had a strange detachment that only he seemed to be capable of in times like this. Sangster was filing it away in the way he was teaching Alex to do. *Pay attention.* That was the rule that applied over all others.

Alex heard a splash as one of the pedestrians fell off the pier into the water. There had to be a hundred people running pell-mell between the three agents and the invaders. He couldn't get a good count of the vampires because they were still bunched up at the back where they climbed onto the pier next to the restaurant, and much of the activity there was obscured by guardrails.

Sangster ran to the end of the pier and leaned over, aiming for the ladder of white latticework that was attached. He began to shoot in rounds of three.

Alex reached the edge of the humans and faced an advancing group of vampires, all with their faces painted. "There's too many."

"Pick one," Armstrong said.

Alex chose a vampire that was thirty yards away and closing in. He pulled the trigger on his Polibow and saw the bolt sizzle and smoke as it struck the vampire in the chest, missing the heart. He fired again, this bolt finding its mark, and the creature exploded.

He aimed at another target that had slowed up as he shot the first. Alex watched the vampire come close to the first and fired, and got lucky. As the first went up he caught the second and they exploded together.

Armstrong was clear of pedestrians now and let loose with rounds from her machine gun.

Then there was an all-new sound, something strange howling from the edge of the pier.

Alex and the two agents stopped, huddling together. In the distance behind them, over the din of screams, they could hear heavy engines, likely Polidorium vehicles moving down the long avenue toward the pier.

But out on the pier there was a loud, echoing, popping sound, like something solid and slightly wet smacking into place, pieces clunking together.

The sound of an engine, heavy and churning, came across the waves. Below the machine-like sound, Alex detected an undercurrent of deep growling, one powered by angry spirits and growing louder.

"Behind the restaurant!" Sangster called Alex's attention to the activity at the far end of the pier. Alex could barely understand what he was seeing emerge from the water, but it was coming fast.

Like grasping fingers, long cords of bone-like white material scuttled out from around the restaurant in jointed, moving sticks. As vampires with skull faces continued to advance, all but ignoring the three agents gathered on the pier, Alex saw the strange bone sticks stack themselves deliberately into shape.

As they found available space on the boards, the bone sticks formed wheels the size of men, then a long, flat chassis, and finally a great coach. In front of the coach, a small set of bones flipped and rolled into place and grew into something that resembled a pair of skeletal horses.

"What the—?" Alex whispered in shock.

A new scream cut him off. A vampire emerged on the roof of the restaurant. Alex recognized the shrieking voice instantly, and as he looked up, he saw the female vampire with blazing yellow hair, her eyes and nose painted over with black. "Now!" she cried, and leapt into the driver's seat of the coach.

"That's Elle," said Alex. Sangster nodded. The vampire called Elle, who looked about sixteen but was possibly hundreds of years old, was well known to the Polidorium. At least by name and reputation: They didn't have much on her background, but Elle seemed to occupy a place of some trust in the Scholomance. She had also been a thorn in Alex's side, assigned to keep tabs on him. Elle whipped the reins and the carriage began to move, great skeletal horse hooves clapping on the boards as they went.

The vampires now formed up around her as the carriage picked up speed.

Sangster whipped his arm over his head. "Fall back."

They broke and ran for their van as Armstrong shouted into the radio, "Farmhouse, they've got a . . ." She took a moment to look at Sangster and then went ahead choosing whatever seemed to come to mind. "They're using some kind of system of vampire magic to power a mock horse-drawn carriage. I think it's made of bone."

"Copy that," came the disconnected voice.

"It might be the same bone spell that they use to reinforce the roof of the Scholomance," Sangster mused as they ran. Alex had seen the vast latticework that stretched for miles inside the organization, creating the structure of its highest ceilings, allowing them to have a sort of cavern that encased a whole city.

"And why does this matter?" Alex asked. He wasn't being sarcastic. If Sangster was bothering to say it, he had a reason.

"Bone work of that sort is not a specialty of the

Scholomance; it would have to be brought in by some-one new," Sangster said as he ran. They reached the van and hunkered behind it and Sangster rapped on the door four times, hard and fast. "It's very rare. Extremely dark power."

Alex glanced around the van, parked in the cobble-stone street like a sitting duck. The carriage was moving at a steady clip now, with the vampires no longer charg-ing on their own but formed up around it. The army of skulls seemed to be jogging beside the carriage, remind-ing him of the parade of a circus.

The van door didn't open. Alex looked at Sangster and ran to the front of the van.

The window of the driver's side was tinted. "Hey!" he yelled.

A hand, red with blood, slapped against the glass, and Alex saw it, darkened and clouded behind the tint-ing. He made out the slumping form of the driver and shrank back as a skull-faced vampire thrust its face against the glass.

Alex shrieked even as he brought up the Polibow, pumping a bolt through the window. The window shat-tered and the creature exploded, fire filling the inside of the van.

Alex staggered back.

Armstrong looked at the smoke pouring out of the van window and opened her hands as if to say, *What'd you have to go and do that for?*

"The—there was a vampire in there."

"How?" screamed Armstrong. "Those doors are protected."

"We left the door cracked so we could fall back into it," Sangster said.

"Okay, okay, new plan," Alex said.

"We are way outnumbered," Sangster said. The sound of the carriage and the incessant, unholy whine of its magic engine came fast with the advance of bone hooves and vampire boots. "Come on, keep moving."

They waited a moment as the army advanced, and Alex watched Elle at the reins, whipping long tendrils of leather, a wild look in her blackened eyes.

As soon as the procession passed, the three followed. There was nothing else they could do until reinforcements arrived.

Halfway up the avenue there was a crowd of people, bunched up near cars that had run into one another and stalled.

When the carriage arrived at the throng of people, they heard the ratcheting sound again. Behind the carriage, more bone rods shot out, latching onto one another and building until it formed a sort of trailer, with white bars.

From the shelter of a shop entrance Alex asked, "What's that?"

"It looks like a cage," Sangster said.

The vampires moved out, this time grabbing people. A man in a leather coat screamed as one of the skull-faced vampires picked him up by the shoulders and threw him. He landed in the cage, rolling across the bumpy floor. They were gathering up captives.

No, no, this is not gonna happen.

Alex heard Sangster yell, "Wait!" but he was already moving.

The darkened street was bedlam, lit up by the glow of lampposts and the glistening bone of the carriage. Alex scanned the street as he ran. He looked up at Elle, who had stopped to yell instructions to the vampires.

Find somewhere high.

Not far from her was the second-story window of a shop, and it had a small balcony with flowerpots. At the edge of that building Alex saw a stalled car that had rammed into a drainage pipe.

Heavy static throbbed in his brain as he cut around the vampires who were grabbing people.

"Alex, get back and wait for backup!" Sangster called.

"I'm going after Elle!" Alex shouted. There was a chance that without their leader in the operation, they might slow down in confusion. It would buy the agents time. Alex leapt onto the hood of the car, which was parked under the store's balcony, and then grabbed a drainpipe at the corner of the building, yanking at it to see if it would hold his weight. Satisfied, he scrambled up until he was across from the balcony.

It was just out of reach.

Six inches. Leap, grab, hold on. Do it now.

His arm sang with pain as he grabbed the rusted metal and swung wild beneath it, his legs churning in the air until he brought them up and stilled himself. He climbed up onto the outside of the balcony railing and began walking sideways along it.

When he was about even with Elle, who was four feet down and fifteen feet out into the street, he brought his Polibow up. He was ready to pump a bolt into her heart as soon as his arm found her chest. He turned to shoot.

Suddenly she was already in midair, a flash of white as she leapt across the distance, hitting him like a sledgehammer to the chest. Her white hands grabbed his throat and he felt weightless for a second. Then the wooden frame and plate glass of the shop's french doors burst apart behind his shoulders, and they tumbled together into a storage room, landing in sacks of flour and glass.

"Alex!" Elle laughed. "I was genuinely wondering when you were gonna show up."

Alex rolled away from her and grabbed a sack of flour, hurling it into her face. It hit her hard and she flipped back, the flour exploding around the room. Alex looked around quickly.

Mixer, metal bowls, flour, sugar, desk, letters, letter opener.

Alex reached for the desk, lifting himself up and grabbing the letter opener. He got to his feet and backed up. He had a stake in his go package, but he would have to reach around for it and she was fast.

Elle took a moment to brush the flour off, waving in the air in front of her.

"This is a new look for you," Alex said.

"Don't you just love it?"

"Is the whole Scholomance dressed up like the Day of the Dead now or just this crew?"

"This is a vanguard, Alex. We're the front line. You are so screwed I can't even tell you."

"Come on!" Alex held out the letter opener. "Elle, what is going on? The Scholomance is supposed to be secret, right? You can't take over a town and keep a low profile."

"I'm sure you'll clean it up." Her legs coiled as she leapt. He thrust up with the letter opener and caught the folds of cloth under her arms. She flipped over him and brought him down to the ground, her arm around his throat. She whispered in his ear as she lifted him up off the ground. She was so incredibly strong. Elle dragged him toward the window. "Look."

Down below, the cage was nearly full of captives. He heard the rumbling of trucks as a pair of Polidorium vans pulled onto the street behind the crowds farther up the avenue.

"Yeah, that's the cavalry," Alex said, his voice raspy from being in a choke hold. There were gunshots now, as agents poured into the streets from the vans. Alex watched puffs of fire go up as skull-faced vampires exploded.

"Aren't you going to ask," Elle whispered, "what it means?"

"What what means? The people, the captives?" Alex said, his mind racing. He felt compelled to play her game, if nothing else, to see if she would relax enough that he could reach into the go package she was smashing him against and grab the handle of his stake. "Are they sacrifices?"

"No." She spoke as if she planned to count his answers.

"Hmm. You're replenishing your stock." Down in

the Scholomance the vampires fed off captives, but they were usually carefully chosen from among people reported missing or otherwise already given up. It would be strange to grab a bunch of people off the street.

"No, for all the reasons you're smart enough to figure out," Elle said, as though she could read his mind.

Alex listened to the whine of the infernal engine of the carriage and the false, panting skeletal horses. The bone power was new, a big deal, Sangster had said. "It's a show. A show of power."

"Not bad," she said.

"But what power?"

"The one you thought you could stop." Elle seemed to shiver for a moment as a reedy, high-pitched call cut through the street, and the procession of vampires below parted.

Alex had his shot. As her body momentarily relaxed, he reached back with his right hand and found the hilt of his special silver-laced stake. He grabbed it and slammed it into her side, the nearest point he could. She shrieked as it hissed against her flesh.

He didn't waste time once she let go of him. Alex climbed over the balcony and jumped, aiming for a skull-faced vampire and hitting him in the back with his knees. Alex rolled to the ground and got up, vampires jostling around him. Everyone seemed to concentrate on the emerging, reedy call.

Then he saw it: As the crowd parted there came a long horse, this one not made of bone but instead somehow worse, alive and elongated, skeletal but stretched with skin. The horse was the length of the carriage Elle had driven.

Riding atop the horse was a figure in white, wearing a thin veil that shimmered in the darkness. One arm gripped a long, narrow, bony scythe.

Beneath the veil he could see a strange white visage, very nearly a skull, with shining glimmers where its eyes should be. It was Claire, the Queen of the Dead.

"It's impossible." Alex spoke into his microphone. "She's supposed to be stuck and unable to come back. They needed my blood."

"Looks like they got what they needed," Sangster guessed.

The Queen swept her arms and Alex started at the sound of a cracking whip. Elle was back in the carriage now, and the Queen remained as Elle guided the carriage toward the marina.

The Queen drew what looked like a reddish spear and threw it to the ground, and Alex watched the staff stick there and vibrate.

After a second it grew taller, flowering out into a wagon-wheel-like shape at the top. The wagon wheel tilted and then began to revolve, suggesting a mechanism.

"It looks like a satellite dish." Alex's brain blazed with powerful energy passing over him as the "dish" swiveled.

A pair of heavily armed Polidorium agents pushed past Alex and aimed at the Queen and began firing. Vampires scattered and the Queen looked down, her skull-like face behind the veil leveling its gaze on them. She rode forward, their bullets pounding against her, sizzling but not exploding.

She whipped the scythe, catching vampires and agents alike. Screams rang out only to be cut short.

Alex moved backward, stumbling and falling to the ground.

He got to his feet and reached back, finding a silver knife and throwing it in one move. The knife bounced off the scythe as it came around, and then the Queen brought it around again, this time to strike him down.

No time to leap, no place to move.

He heard another high-pitched whine, like a motorcycle.

The scythe came sweeping down and a four-foot-long

green staff flashed before his eyes, coming from nowhere. The metal staff parried the scythe's blow, and the Queen jolted her head sideways in surprise.

Alex felt someone grab him by the collar and pull him back, and a green motorcycle of no make he had ever seen before whipped around and in front of him.

The rider wore a blue helmet and was obviously female, wearing a light-colored jacket over her thin frame. Her back turned to Alex, the rider shrieked at the Queen in a language he couldn't identify.

Suddenly the figure cried in English, "*Traitor!*"

Silence. The Queen brought her free hand up to her scythe and touched her fingers, almost shrugging. There was a hint of merriment in her blazing veiled eyes.

"No *traitor*," she said thickly, in English. "Triumphant."

Something in the air popped, and Alex felt light filtering into his eyes from above. A great hole had opened where the dark curtain of night was retracting, and light clouds crossed the daytime sky as the great reddish horse turned, and the Queen galloped toward the lake like a fluid and screaming ghost. The last of the vampires that had not retreated with Elle's carriage went with the skull-headed lady, surrounding the horse and moving just as fast. Within moments, the streets were empty of the dead and gleamed with sunlight.

All that remained were the Polidorium agents and the rider of the green motorcycle, which churned with a muffled softness as near-organic as the engine of the Queen's carriage. Alex saw that other than handlebars, the bike was devoid of controls.

The girl on the bike flipped her staff and it collapsed to about a foot long, and she stuck it in a saddlebag.

"Who are you?" Alex asked. But already he had a suspicion, an inkling he could not explain.

The girl took off her helmet, turned her head, and smiled. It was Astrid.

CHAPTER 6

The avenue was awash in radio chatter as Sangster and Alex approached Astrid. "Who are you?" Sangster asked again, yanking off his gas mask. Alex was stunned and silent.

"Astrid Gretelian. I'm here about Claire."

"About *Claire*?" Sangster repeated the name incredulously. "How did you even know there was a Claire?"

She looked around as though it might not be safe to talk. Sangster cast a glance back at the restaurant behind them. The door was open and he nodded in that direction. They began to walk, Astrid keeping her distance as she rolled her bike. Sangster shouted into his Bluetooth to the others.

"See if there are any vampires left in the village. I doubt it because of the sunlight, but make sure there aren't any hiding indoors. Armstrong? Get with communications; find out what the deal was with that dish thing."

The three of them gathered in the restaurant and stood next to a brick wall, surrounded by empty tables with white linens. Some of them had been overturned.

"All right, Astrid Gretelian," Sangster said. "Answers."

"You don't have to talk to me that way." Astrid frowned. "I just saved your friend."

"Who are you?"

"I'm Astrid—"

"She's new at school," Alex interrupted. "I met her this morning. She said she's from the Netherlands, and I think that's right." He watched the girl with a mixture of distrust and admiration. She had saved his life, surely, but this morning she had pretended to be . . . what? Had she pretended anything at all?

"And she's a witch," Sangster said evenly.

A witch. Alex took the word like a slap to the face even though it wasn't aimed at him, because it was the second time that word had come into his life in any real, magical way in a short time. His mother was a witch.

Alex thought of his mother, Amanda, who had the

tall, blond model good looks of a Swedish pop star—the same good looks his own twin sister had, but of which he judged he had inherited precisely none. His mom was many things—a charitable organizer, a professor sometimes, a deft manager of five children, and through it all she carried an ironic and whimsical tone that seemed to armor her against any kind of upset. She could be funny and sometimes cruel, but she was loving.

And yes, a witch, and not the let-me-figure-out-who-you're-going-to-marry-with-this-Ouija-board kind, but a let-me-shut-these-windows-with-my-mind kind. But Amanda had given up an active life of witchcraft when she had married an agent of the Polidorium, Alex's dad.

Astrid was a witch like his mother. She had beaten back the Queen with magic words and swung a weapon that didn't act like anything he'd ever seen.

But Alex didn't sense any static coming off Astrid. If she were evil, somehow, if she were something dark, wouldn't his brain be buzzing?

He looked at her again, his eyes suddenly widening. *Holy crap, do you know my mom?*

"What is Claire?" Sangster asked, bringing Alex back to reality. Alex wasn't sure if Sangster was testing her or trying to figure out the real answer.

"Claire Clairmont," Astrid said. "Born in 1798, half

sister of Mary Shelley and lover of Lord Byron."

"And according to history, she died an old spinster governess," Sangster added.

Astrid put her bony hands on her hips, looking impatient. "Well, according to history, John Polidori died a feeble drug addict in 1821, but we *know better*, don't we?"

Sangster betrayed no emotion, but Alex knew the gears in Sangster's head had to be turning as much as his own were. The fact that John Polidori, a British writer who had first identified Lord Byron as a vampire, had gone underground and founded the organization they worked for was far from common knowledge. How could she know this? But by itself it didn't prove anything; even Minhi knew that much about the Polidorium, and Astrid had spent the night talking to Minhi.

Astrid went on. "Claire Clairmont was obsessed with Lord Byron, and after his death traveled to Russia in the 1820s. There she allowed herself to be recruited based on the power of her inborn abilities to seduce, and she learned the magical arts. But it was all for her own purposes: she wanted eternal life, with Byron, with whom she made an undead, unholy pact. She made him a more powerful vampire and sacrificed herself. But at the right time, he would revive her and they would rule together."

"Rule together?" Sangster seemed to be trying to

decide whether he found that plausible. "Yeah, lemme throw out history again. Byron hated Claire."

"Well." Alex shrugged, but that was as far as he got.

"Oh, please." Astrid turned to her reflection in a large glass wine jug against the wall and started unraveling one of her pigtails and rebanding it. As she held a rubber band in her mouth she went on. "Are you going to stand there and tell me that Lord Byron himself did not just three months ago attempt to resurrect Claire to be the Queen of the Vampires?"

Alex turned to Sangster with his hands open, as if to say, *So she knows everything.* "But that didn't work," Alex said. "Byron failed and he's locked away. And then Byron's disciple, Elle, tried her damnedest to get my blood to finish resurrecting her, and *she* failed."

"Wait, she needed your blood, why?" Astrid asked.

Alex glanced at Sangster—was this secret? Did it matter? Sangster nodded and Alex continued. "Byron used some of my blood to start bringing Claire back from a pile of bones he'd summoned. But he didn't get enough, so Elle came for more."

"And that wasn't enough, either?" Astrid kept her eyes on the glass jar, then took another pigtail apart and twisted it, splaying the rubber bands in her fingers. Her accent was so . . . odd and yet normal, just a hint of non-English, causing *enough* to come out *ee-nahff.*

"Well, I mean, I didn't let her actually have any of it. It's not free."

Astrid chuckled, a high, cheery laugh that snorted out quickly as she finished rebanding the last stray pigtail. She tilted her head, surveying all of them in the curvature of the giant jug. "So it looks like they managed anyway—maybe they took a sample of your blood while you were sleeping?"

Sangster rubbed the back of his neck and turned to Alex, considering it. "Wouldn't have to be blood. They have labs at the Scholomance; they might have used your DNA. All it would take is a strand of hair."

"Not a strand of hair," Alex said, sighing. "I lost a contact case with my lenses in town a few weeks ago. There could have been stuff on the lenses."

"Right." Astrid smiled awkwardly. "So however they got it, they got your DNA and used it to finish raising Claire. And now she's back. And let me tell you, the moment she hit this realm, we heard about it. And I was sent to look into it."

"We?" Alex asked. "Who's we?"

Armstrong stuck her head through the front door of the restaurant. "Sangster? Come look at this."

They followed her to the Polidorium van that still sat in the center of the road. Inside, a technician was attaching long cables to a computer panel he'd opened in the side door. Over his head, on the screen, two lines shimmered. Alex did not recognize the language.

Sangster looked around, then at Astrid. "Can you read that?"

She shook her head. "No."

"You spoke a language to Claire. Was it this one?"

"I spoke the language of Dulle Grit," she said.

"What's Dulle Grit?" Alex asked.

"Dulle Grit is *fascinating*." Astrid's shoulders bobbed with excitement, and she momentarily returned to the girl he had met a few hours before. "You're going to love—"

Sangster held up a hand. "Save that for study hall, okay? So you spoke a language shared by your organization."

"Doesn't *your* organization have a language?"

"English."

"Ours is a little older." Astrid looked at the words. "But this isn't Hexen verbiage. This is . . . coded."

"Wait, wait, wait," Alex said. "Who's the *we* you said, who's your organization?" This was very strange.

"Hexen," Sangster answered before Astrid could open her mouth again. "She works for an organization called Hexen."

"See? Aren't you glad we met?" Astrid said, touching him on the shoulder. "You're going to need my help."

"I've never heard of Hexen." Alex eyed her warily.

"That surprises me."

"Why?"

"He's new," Sangster explained. "But I don't understand. We haven't heard from Hexen in years. And as I recall you want it that way."

"We protect the world in very different ways."

"And they sent you to beat back an invasion from the Skull-Headed Lady? What are you, fourteen?"

Alex and Astrid both stared.

Armstrong talked more to the engineer than to them. "We can get these lines analyzed. We'll figure out what it says. The Queen showed up and sent us a message. She won't make it impossible to read."

"Oh, hold on." Astrid held out her hands excitedly. "Maybe I can do this." She reached into a pocket and drew out a small bead, very light and waxy looking, like a soft jelly bean.

"What's that?"

"It's a spell. We prepare our tools with spells beforehand because sometimes they can get complicated and it's useful to . . . how would you say it?—concentrate them in the field. But I might be able to use it."

"You have a code-cracking spell in a jelly bean?" Alex asked.

"Not so much; it's a spell of seeing—you know, in

case someone's around a corner. But it might be close enough."

She whispered something into the small bead and blew on it, and Alex watched the ephemeral material fly with her breath toward the screen and fluff away into nothing.

Astrid bounced expectantly. "I love puzzles."

The green lines shimmered briefly and started to change, but then the screen went dark and cloudy. After a moment it returned, and Astrid frowned and harrumphed.

Armstrong nodded. "We'll give it a shot."

"Good, because I only have one of those."

Alex was looking out into the street. Civilians were moving about, beginning to sweep up. An air of calm had taken over, and the place looked like it had been hit by a storm, nothing more. "What now?"

Sangster thought for a moment. "You're undercover in the school?" he asked Astrid.

"Yes."

"When do you have to report in?"

"Tonight."

"Okay," Sangster said. "I'm taking the day off. I'll call in sick. You two need to go back to the school."

"What?" Astrid cried. "We don't know what she's planning."

"Look," said the teacher. "I don't know how you work, but do you understand that you've put us at risk? If your cover is blown, Alex's could be, too. Until we have a chance to sort this out, you both need to get back."

"Those are not my instructions."

"Yeah, but are you here to cooperate with us or not?" Sangster demanded.

"With all due respect," she replied, "I'm here to make sure you don't foul this up."

Sangster actually laughed. "Right. Right. Of course." He looked at Alex. "Keep her out of trouble. You're gonna be late, so the story is that you decided to cut class together."

"What?" Alex asked. His mind spun. That wasn't something he did every day. Plus another thought that didn't have any business there at all.

"Just if anyone asks. Reveal her nature to no one. You liked her, you went for a ride. I'm not causing an incident between us and Hexen within four hours of contact. The story is simple and it works; you have an iffy reputation anyway."

"I'm *working on* my reputation," Alex responded. "What the heck kind of thing is that for a teacher to say?"

"Cut me some slack." Sangster paused and looked at

them both. "Midnight. Farmhouse."

"You're letting her in the farmhouse?"

"She could get in the farmhouse on her own," Sangster said. Astrid shrugged.

Alex thought maybe that was the case and maybe it was not. Maybe she had another jelly bean that would open the false tin door in the front of the old house in the woods, the one that took you into a path that led a mile down into an underground bunker, or maybe she was not so prepared. Sangster clearly had decided that she was something to be treated gingerly.

Alex raised a hand. "I have a question. How are we getting back?"

Astrid turned to him. "You want a ride?"

CHAPTER 7

Alex rode to Glenarvon-LaLaurie on the back of Astrid's motorcycle, which seemed to be a modified Italian design that she handled with expert efficiency.

Alex kept his fingers locked at Astrid's waist as they rode, and he tried to process her presence in Secheron. Too much was happening too fast for him to follow it all. The girl had come into the school, bouncy and brash and strange, and all along she had been harboring a secret—a secret mission, in fact. There was nothing to hang on to here, he felt, nothing to trust. And Sangster had handed Alex over to her care as if everyone knew that she wasn't a thrall, like Vienna Cazorla had been— a servant of the Scholomance, out to betray them. No one could know if that were the case. And yet here they were.

And the bike—the strangest thing about Astrid's motorcycle was not the complete lack of controls but rather the unearthly sound the engine made, which he couldn't get used to. She had almost parked it in front of the school before he had advised her that the proper way to deal with your undercover transportation was to stash it in the woods, which she did, right next to his own motorcycle.

"A Kawasaki Ninja." She watched Alex drag several rough-cut limbs and cover up both bikes. "You go to a lot of trouble to hide what you are."

Alex blinked. "I don't think so." He watched her standing there, her hands clasped together. He had a thousand questions and no idea where to start.

Astrid shrugged and began walking, and Alex followed. When they reached the school, they went in through separate doors. Alex waited in the stairwell for the bell to ring, and at three P.M. he made his way into his European History class.

He slid into his seat next to Sid, who brightened but also shook his head with an apparent array of questions.

A moment later, Paul and Minhi came in, holding hands briefly before they separated, Paul next to Sid and Minhi in front of them. Just his luck he had all three of his friends in one class. He prayed class would start before he had to get into the whole business about Secheron.

Minhi turned and looked at him. "I thought you were just going to be gone during lunch."

"Yeah, it, uh, went long."

The door opened and Astrid came in, finding a seat at the far end of the class. She waved at them and smiled. Alex watched her sit and then turned back to Minhi, who looked like she was doing math in her head, sizing up Alex's story.

Alex asked brightly, "How are things going with, uh, Astrid?"

"I don't know. She's been missing for a couple of hours." The same distrust. *Minhi would make a crackerjack detective,* Alex thought.

Paul was listening and pursed his lips. "No *way.*" He laughed, his giant frame shaking. "Is that where . . . Blimey. Nice."

"Come on." Alex opened his hands. *"What?"*

Minhi looked at him more coldly than he felt he probably deserved as the teacher came in and put him out of his misery.

As Alex melted into the rhythm of class, he felt

again the strangeness of a double life. Only hours ago, he had been nearly cut in half by a skull-headed lady on horseback, and now he was listening to something about the start of World War I that he could barely find the needed concentration to follow. He felt the mantle of Student Alex slide over him, and he forced all thoughts of the undead into the recesses of his mind as he opened his history book and began to take notes.

At dinner, the four friends met up in the cafeteria, taking their seats near high windows that looked out onto the grounds.

Astrid joined them, and this time her kiss on Minhi's cheek was met rather more slowly than it had been in the morning.

They chatted as Astrid sketched in a notebook, peppering Minhi with questions about LaLaurie.

All through dinner and after, Alex kept looking out the window, as if he could spot the skull-faced army that had melted away after the attack. Astrid put down her pencil and looked out, observing to the others, "It should be snowing soon. The woods will be lovely. You're so lucky to be here."

Minhi nodded. "It will be lovely! You'll see. I can take

you out in the morning if you want to see the woods before the snow."

"Oh, I have, when we walked this afternoon," Astrid said excitedly. She cast her eyes at Alex. "We spent hours exploring. Alex is a gallant tour guide."

"Ah," Minhi said evenly. "Yeah, that's what my old roommate said."

Alex briefly considered pounding his head against the table but decided it wouldn't help. It was the story, after all. "I'm getting a soda," he said, rising and walking to the back of the room.

At the drink dispensers, in the upper end of the cafeteria where the kitchen had been closed and the shadows were growing long, Minhi appeared next to him.

"So *you* move fast." Minhi busied herself getting a glass of orange juice.

"It's not really like that," Alex said.

"Oh? So you *didn't* cut class with a girl you just met this morning?"

"No, I—well, yeah, but it was . . ." He looked at Minhi. Her brown eyes were wide and expectant. "Um, there was something you wanted to . . . ask. Before I left earlier."

She watched him for what seemed like a long time. "I don't know," she said finally. "It's probably not the time."

"Stop," he said.

"Stop what?"

"Your juice, it's overflowing," he said, pointing to her glass.

"Oh!" Minhi turned and pulled the glass away from the dispenser. "God, I'm so *stupid.*"

"No," Alex said. This was all wrong. "No, it's . . . let's go back."

"To what?" Minhi's mouth curled into a thin frown.

"Okay," Alex said. "Look. I can't keep being jealous."

"What?"

"Don't . . ." He searched for words, looking back at the table. "You know what I mean. I don't know what else to say, but I can't keep being jealous of you and one of my best friends, and, Minhi, you can't keep encouraging me to be. Okay?"

She stopped and looked at him for a long time. Then she said, "Okay. I get it."

"Yeah? Okay?"

"Okay," Minhi said definitively.

Alex nodded. "So we're done with this?"

"We're done." Minhi nodded. Then she smiled, smirking at him. "You really do think you're something."

"It's only what everybody tells me."

They went back to the table and sat, and Paul reached for Minhi's hand.

Minhi looked down at a sketch Astrid was absently making on a napkin with her pen: the tall staff with the circular dish, the horse with the scythe-wielding skeletal figure. Minhi tapped it. "That's interesting. Are you drawing *The Triumph of Death*?"

Alex looked at her. "The what?"

"*The Triumph of Death*," Minhi said. "The painting."

"Triumph," Alex repeated. The Queen had spoken that very word—no, but close to it, she'd said *Triumphant* when Astrid had challenged her.

"Yeah, it's kind of amazing. You should check it out," Minhi said.

Sid started to say something when Alex held up a finger. "Do you have an image of it?"

Minhi seemed to suddenly engage, tilting her head as if she could tell he was thinking something important. As she reached down and pulled a tablet computer out of her bag, Alex felt a mix of emotions—excitement that Minhi might help shed some light on the events of the day, and intense relief after the conversation they'd just had. Like maybe they could go back to being normal.

Minhi brought the tablet to life and spoke into a microphone symbol. "*Triumph of Death*, painting." She lay the tablet down as a series of images appeared on screen, and she expanded one of them to fill the whole display.

The image that filled the screen, though, was a horrific nightmare. Alex's eyes widened as he took in the painting.

The Triumph of Death illustrated in monstrous detail the slaughter of humankind by an army of skeletal beings: the army of death itself.

Across the foreground of the painting, people ran from skeletons that trampled them, cutting their throats, choking them, and dragging them away. A whole slew of people were being herded into a holding cell, like a huge cage or trailer. Dogs chewed on the remains of the fallen. In the distance, ships smoked on the water and cities burned. A great leader of the skeletons, astride a bone-thin, reddish horse, swung an enormous scythe: Death. Alex saw again and again the shock and horror on the faces of the people, their mouths open in cries of agony and despair. All around in the background of the painting was black destruction, buildings and ships burning, little specks of fire floating on the wind.

"Oh my God," Alex whispered under his breath as he started running his fingers over the painting, zooming in and scanning across. *The Triumph of Death* looked like the scene that he had just observed on the curtain of night that surrounded the town of Secheron.

"What is it about?"

"Death wins," Minhi said. "Death has dominion over all."

Dotting the scene were tall staffs with circular wheel-like constructions on the top, very much like the satellite dish–type device the Queen had used. Alex tapped those and looked at Minhi. "What are these?"

She shrugged. "Who knows? In the painting they're used as gallows to hang people on."

This was unreal. The vampires were copying a painting, exactly as it appeared.

Alex looked into Astrid's eyes and she seemed to reflect back his own thoughts.

We are in trouble.

CHAPTER 8

Back in his room, Alex could barely contain his need to get back to the Polidorium, and he paced the floor until it was time. Paul and Sid were still awake when he snuck out to, as Paul put it, "go protect us all from art history."

The woods across from Glenarvon-LaLaurie were pitch black at 11:45 P.M. Alex stood in darkness and watched the condensation of his breath cross the thin crescent moon in the sky beyond the trees. He lit up his watch to check the time. Astrid wasn't there.

Alex wasn't going to wait for her. Possibly she had gotten caught trying to sneak out or disappeared into whatever cave she had emerged from that morning, but as he stood next to his bike, he tried to make any sense out of Sangster's curious deference to her. That deference was because she claimed to represent an organization Alex did not know existed.

"Hexen," Alex muttered aloud, shaking his head.

"That's right," said Astrid as she stepped out of the shadows, her pale face barely visible in the darkness. "What about Hexen?"

"Just that I've never heard of it until today."

"Alex, I really don't want to keep you in the dark." Astrid looked genuine and sweet in the speckled moonlight, and he distrusted her even more. The sunnier she acted, the more clouded his vision of her became. She must be keeping secrets under that pout-like smile. "What do you want to know?"

Alex wanted to say *Everything,* but that would have sounded desperate. He didn't know if he wanted to know everything anyway. He wanted to know everything so he could dismiss it again and go back to a world of him and the Polidorium and no weird, sudden Hexen girl, and while they were at it, no upset Minhi. Not that that was even his problem. It was Paul's problem, wasn't it?

"I don't know." He shook his head. "Whatever's necessary, I guess, but right now we don't have time."

"I'm very sorry to keep you waiting. I had to make sure everyone in the girls' dorm was asleep. So do you want me to follow you?"

"Why don't you ride with *me* this time?" Alex asked Astrid. She had her own helmet but he held an extra Polidorium helmet forward. "Take this one so we can hear one another."

Astrid put on the helmet as he got on the Ninja. Alex indicated the seat behind him as he slid on his goggles and the helmet and tapped a button on the side. Inside his goggles, the trees lit up bright white against the dark spaces of the infrared. Alex started the Ninja, and spoke into a mike inside the helmet.

"Can you hear me?"

"Yes," she replied. "You Polidori really are about the technology. Aren't you going to use headlights?"

"Just put your arms around my . . ."

But she already had, her bony arms folding around him and clasping together at his stomach. Even through the jackets, she felt warm. He throttled the Ninja and took off into the woods.

With Astrid behind him, Alex threaded the motorcycle through the forest, picking up speed as he went. Unnaturally white trees zipped past on either side.

He became aware of the vibration in Astrid's helmet before he heard her erupt in laughter. "You really know these woods!"

"Believe me, if I were starting from anywhere else but the school I'd need the GPS." The bike jolted as it went over some fallen branches. "But by now I have this route down. Should be just a few minutes."

After a while he saw a clearing of darkness beyond the trees, and then the glowing image of a building.

They broke through the tree line and the farmhouse came into view, a small, unassuming shack with a battered sheet-metal garage door to the side. The moment they passed into the clearing, as the wheels began to churn over soft earth, Alex saw tiny red lights shining, cameras perched overhead in the trees beyond the clearing, watching their progress.

Astrid gasped, the sound echoing in his ear as he gunned the engine and headed straight for the sheet-metal door. As he drew within a few yards, it swung up fast, and he zipped inside.

Track lights came on as they moved on to a concrete drive at a thirty-degree grade, and now more obvious cameras swung toward him.

They passed wooden beams and swiftly responding gun emplacements that swiveled and idled, vibrating on their struts as the Ninja moved past. Down, down, half a mile, until they emerged into a giant concrete hangar, moving past trucks with helicopters on the backs of them and all manner of vehicles.

"This," said Alex, "is the farmhouse."

He came to a stop next to a bike he recognized as Sangster's black Triumph Speed Triple with the Polidorium emblem on the back of the seat.

Astrid looked around as she took off her helmet. For once, she seemed impressed. Alex led her up the metal stairs at the back and through a door. They stepped into the carpeted corridor, past offices of agents working at computer screens and drawing on enormous glass maps. "I had no idea."

Alex shrugged and turned the boardroom door handle. "Well, we gotta work somewhere."

Inside, Alex found Sangster and Armstrong bent over an enormous table with the Polidorium legend *Talia sunt* set into the shiny black surface. They were looking at a wall screen, and Sangster invited Alex and Astrid to sit.

"Minhi was right," Sangster said. "It *is The Triumph of Death.*"

Alex smiled slightly. He had called Sangster about Minhi's suggestion as soon as he'd had a chance. "Fantastic. She showed us the painting in a book, too."

"Okay. Let's talk about the painter. Pieter Bruegel." Sangster indicated the screen. Projected on the wall Alex saw two images: a picture of a painter, bearded with a floppy sort of hood, like a medieval worker might wear, and some key biographical data. The second image was the painting itself.

"Bruegel was Flemish," Sangster reported. "He painted *The Triumph of Death* sometime around 1562. We don't have an exact date."

Alex looked at the individual parts of the painting and focused in on the image of what looked like a satellite dish. He remembered it had sent a message. "And it's amazing. Could the Queen be using this as a, I don't know, a screenplay for what she was doing this afternoon?"

"More like the opposite, but we'll get to that," Sangster said.

Armstrong tapped a key in an invisible keyboard in the tabletop and brought up the coded message that had been beamed into the van. "Bruegel was the key to deciphering the coded message that Claire sent. We were pretty sure that because Claire was a member of Hexen, that she would use the Hexen language."

"She hasn't been one of us for a *very* long time," Astrid said. "I just want to make that clear."

"Noted," Armstrong said, nodding. "Anyway, this coded message she sent was in gibberish, just symbols.

But all codes have a key, a way to start mapping one alphabet against another. Like I said, we knew that the Hexen language—or Dulle Grit, as you called it, a language developed in secret by the founders of Hexen deriving from a form of Druidic—was likely to be the language that we would be translating into. The key-word we used to decode the message was *Bruegel*. That got us to this."

The image changed to show a new stream of letters, and this time Astrid's eyes lit up with recognition. "That's Hexen."

Armstrong nodded. "Right, so that's the Hexen version . . . and this is the English." She pressed a button.

This time the words shifted and glowed there. Alex read them with a sinking feeling.

WHAT IS LOST WILL BE FOUND.

YOU HAVE SEVEN DAYS UNTIL SUNSET.

"Seven days until sunset?" Alex asked.

"Here's what we think," said Sangster. "The Queen has gotten hold of a very powerful spell that can plunge the world into darkness, which she demonstrated amply this afternoon in Secheron. She's threatening to use it in a big way, even taunting us by showing us the picture."

Astrid seemed surprised. "You've heard of this spell?"

Sangster nodded. "Polidori left copious notes on the

various magicks that the vampires picked up and trafficked in while he was alive. This one is called a lot of things, such as *Obscura Notte*, Dimmer Switch. And of course, the Triumph of Death."

"This would be completely forbidden. We're not supposed to do stuff like that." Astrid shook her head emphatically. "She's going to need a week just to build up the reserve energy to do it."

"You said 'forbidden'?" Alex was trying to get a feel for how the witches were organized. He wished his mom had been more forthcoming about her powers. He wanted to ask Astrid if his mother had been a member of Hexen, but set it aside. There were more pressing issues. "So, what, you have laws?"

"Of course. Magic is about the use of the spirit. It takes energy," Astrid said. "It's one thing if you're helping, if you're in spirit with the earth, if you're going with the natural flow of things. Those spells increase everyone's energy. The world welcomes it. But conflict is harder. Huge spells that torment and cause pain to masses of people are costly to us. Pain leaves an ugly mark on the world. It's not what magic is for. A spell like this is nothing but torment. It takes something out of everybody. But we suspected that Claire would want to do something like this."

Alex studied the painting. "So the painting is a sort of model for the Triumph."

Sangster shook his head. "Like I said, it goes the other way. We think the painting is a sort of report of the spell. A warning. Except that Bruegel was painting in the sixteenth century, long before there *was* a Polidorium, so he didn't do it for us. But there were other organizations back then. Polidori made reference to an Order that we know Bruegel dealt with. We think the painting is a message left for us if we ever had to deal with the Triumph. But I was gonna say, there's a problem."

"What?" Alex asked, turning toward Sangster.

Sangster brought up the database that Alex had seen numerous times, a huge index with a search bar.

Armstrong typed in "Dimmer Switch" and the entry came up, followed by its various other names. Alex saw "Triumph of Death" among them. Next, where he should have seen an article, Alex saw three words.

File not found.

"Where's the file? What happened?" Alex asked.

"It was deleted," Sangster said, "by a virus that shot through our systems. We think the way it worked is through a wireless connection coming from one of our mobile data devices. You get one guess when."

"This morning," Alex said. "They used the device

they stole from the plane."

Astrid had a quizzical look, and Alex quickly told her about the vampires that had hijacked his plane and taken the study computer.

"What about backups?" Alex asked.

"All erased. We do have notes on Bruegel and his painting, but not much of that."

"So the Scholomance is using a spell that Polidori left us instructions on how to deal with, but they erased what we have. Where does that leave us?"

"It leaves us with seven days to figure it out all over again." Sangster turned to Astrid. "What about Hexen? Do they have anything on this?"

She shook her head. "Not really. Most of the information on Claire was handed over by Brelaz during the Summit."

"The Summit?" Alex could hear the capital letter. "Who the heck is Brelaz?"

"Madame Brelaz was a Portuguese agent of Hexen and a friend of Polidori," Sangster explained. "She helped Polidori go underground. At that time, early in Polidori's secret life, they were sharing a lot of information, and there was some hope on Hexen's part that a new, heavily scientific arm of Hexen might be created."

"But Polidori turned his back on the use of magic,"

Astrid said. "And there hasn't been much cooperation between Hexen and the Polidorium since the mid-1800s."

"Why is there always something else that I don't know?" Alex asked.

"That's what makes life magical," Astrid said brightly.

Alex stared at Astrid and shook his head, turning his attention back to the message. "'WHAT IS LOST WILL BE FOUND.' What's that a reference to?"

"We're not sure. Icemaker, maybe," Sangster guessed.

"Who?" Astrid asked.

"It's what we call Byron," Alex explained.

"So where is Byron, currently?" Astrid continued.

Everyone was silent for a moment. Alex hadn't been told where Byron was, either, though he figured he had some right to know. After all, it had been Alex who had managed to clap his hand down on the liquid nitrogen system that had frozen and encased the vampire in ice.

"We're keeping him safe," Sangster said.

Armstrong added, "And we're absolutely not handing him over to Claire."

Astrid laughed, that same eruption she had let out on the motorcycle. "No, no! I agree."

"Well, I'm glad *you* agree," Alex said before he could stop himself. Couldn't she be less positive? Please?

And did she have to act like she was on an even level with Sangster and Armstrong? Alex had been here for months and he didn't dare do that.

"Wait!" Astrid said, looking back at the painting. "Of *course.*"

"What?" Alex asked.

"The spell, the Dimmer Switch as you call it, is literally the Triumph of Death. It will allow Claire to control the dead. Even those in the earth."

"And she could find anyone dead." Sangster nodded, following. "She casts the spell and it's not just that she can scare everybody and let vampires run around all day. She might be able to raise the dead as well and command an army of death."

"Zombies," Alex said. "The Scholomance had a few zombie guards in their main tunnel."

"These would be summoned dead, new zombies. It's not a skill everyone has. Dracula can do it, but everyone else would need a big spell like this."

"We don't know the extent of the necromantic powers that could be bestowed once she unleashes the spell," Astrid said.

Alex drummed his fingers. "Okay. Big spell, big power, and she leaves a hint. Why? Why is she giving us a chance to stop it?" Alex asked.

Sangster paused. "We don't know."

Alex sat back. "So . . . where do we start?"

"Look for a heavy convergence of ley lines," Astrid said.

"What?" Alex looked at her. "What lines?"

"Ley lines," Astrid repeated. "Think of them as longitude and latitude for the magical realm. But there are more of them in some places, and those places make good spots for setting off major spells. We're talking about Stonehenge, Rome, New Orleans."

Alex brightened. "Hey, maybe we get to go to New Orleans."

"Let's back up a moment," said Armstrong. "It's now midnight on the night after a plane you were riding was hijacked, resulting in the loss of a computer that has now put the Polidorium at risk."

Alex felt the blood prickle in his cheeks. "I . . . you know that's not my fault."

"I'm just saying that this is serious, Alex. This is a *major* threat. We haven't made assignments for this project."

"What about Hexen?" Sangster changed the subject, looking at Astrid. "You said you were here to look into Claire."

"Yes."

"So now you've looked. Can I assume that your organization is going to continue working on this?"

"I think you can assume that."

"And can I assume that a more experienced operative will be representing Hexen going forward?"

Astrid looked as if she'd been struck. "No. This is my project."

"Is it possible you could set up a meeting—"

Alex looked at Sangster in shock. Sangster, who had personally guided Alex for the past several months, was clearly suggesting that Astrid and Alex were too young and inexperienced for this. He wasn't even sure he liked Astrid, but this was not like Sangster.

"Absolutely not," Astrid protested. "Hexen has made its decision."

"And I'm supposed to just take your word for that?"

"No, of course not." Astrid smiled in a pouting way as though assuaging a child. She reached into her pocket, and for a split second Alex thought she was going to draw a weapon. But instead she brought out a piece of jewelry, a silver chain flashing in the air. She slapped her fist down on the table and opened it, revealing the object that lay there.

Alex had no frame of reference for this, but Sangster slowly leaned forward. In the center of the table was a cameo, a delicately curved portrait on a pendant.

"May I . . . ?" he asked, and reached out his hand.

"Of course."

Sangster picked up the pendant and looked at it, holding it up to the light. "This is the Brelaz cameo."

Astrid nodded. "Given in friendship by Dr. John Polidori to Madame Brelaz in 1819. Do you know what it means?"

Alex shook his head.

Sangster said, "It gives its bearer the full weight of Hexen authority and the right to speak for the organization should the two ever cross again."

Armstrong let out a slow whistle. "That has not been seen in . . . what . . ."

"Seventy-five years?" Sangster estimated. He slid it back and raised his hands. "Okay, okay, I surrender. Your papers appear to be in order. Hexen doesn't call and doesn't write for nearly a century, and now we get you."

"For now," Astrid said. "For Claire."

"Because you guys think of Claire as *your* problem," Armstrong said.

"We think she's everybody's problem."

"Any other orders in there we should know about?"

"There is something else." Astrid gestured toward Alex with her head. "With all gentle kindness, I'm not here to work with you. I'm supposed to work with him."

Alex wasn't sure she was pointing at him at first. That seemed absurd. *Hey, I was just starting to hate you.*

Sangster cocked his head and looked at the two of them. Alex opened his hands as if to say, *Don't look at me.* "What does that mean exactly?"

"That's enough for now," Astrid said. "But if I'm working with the Polidorium, I'm working with Van Helsing."

Sangster breathed slowly. "Well, we were gonna bring Alex anyway. He's not bad at all this."

"Thanks," said Alex.

"But he has a terrible reputation." Sangster smiled.

"So." Alex leaned back. "I gotta ask again. Now that I'm the number-one-requested single, where do we start?"

Sangster shrugged. "We start with the painting, *The Triumph of Death.* We know it's a key, but thanks to the computer virus, we don't have the Polidorium's notes on it, so we need to look at it more closely."

"Where is this painting?" Astrid asked.

Sangster scrolled through the data under the painting. "It's now in the Prado Museum in Madrid, Spain." He leaned back and expertly flipped a pen between his fingers as he looked at Alex and Astrid. "Want to go on a field trip?"

CHAPTER 9

"I actually prefer to fly, Alex." Armstrong turned a fresh, freckled face toward him as she brought the dark gray Polidorium Learjet 60XR to cruising speed.

Alex spent the first five minutes of the flight leaning into the cockpit pestering the pilot. In this case it was Armstrong, the same agent he had seen wearing a U.S. Air Force uniform numerous times and who had already informed him that she was a pilot, so this wasn't really a surprise.

She spoke a few words to the silent copilot and turned back to Alex. "So, we have three hours to Madrid. You're on a fourteen-million-dollar aircraft, and your only chaperone is Sangster, who, seriously, is not the most responsible guardian. The night is young. Go talk to the girl."

"What are you telling him?" asked Sangster, who turned up beside Alex next to the cockpit door. Alex looked back to see Astrid, who was seated alone, poring over an art book. Sangster was wearing his usual outfit for when he wasn't actually rappelling off anything: chinos and a sport coat, so that he always seemed to look like some cross between a spy and a record producer. He ran his hand along the doorframe. "Regs say we should shut this door."

"I think Alex is worried that one of us is a secret vampire," Armstrong said.

"You could be a banana leaf woman," Alex joked.

"Come on." Sangster turned to his protégé, put his hand on his shoulder, and led Alex firmly back toward the seats. "You need to get some rest. It's a big day at the Prado, and you can't waste the time available for sleep."

"I actually am totally fine with, like, no sleep." Thanks to his dad, this was also true.

"Oh, I know." Sangster nodded. "But you jumped out of a plane twenty-four hours ago, you can't possibly have gotten much sleep last night, and we're just getting started. You've earned your points; don't be a hero about naptime."

They stopped next to a tray of drinks and Alex got himself some water. "I was thinking I should send a text to, you know, Paul and Sid and Minhi."

Sangster shook his head. "I don't think that'll work."

"When we land, I mean." But he already knew what Sangster was saying.

"Alex, you can't let your friends in on everything we do." The teacher shrugged. "It's not safe, for them or for you. They already know way more than is safe. You know, I have friends and relatives I wish I could text every time I go somewhere interesting. But it's just not how it works."

Alex's heart sank as he realized that indeed he had already cost his friends mightily—they had been threatened with death by fire, kidnapping, stabbing, and rending limb from limb by vampires. Still . . .

"The thing is that they don't . . ." Alex tried to find the right words. "They're gonna wake up, and I'm not gonna be there. And, you know, *Astrid*'s not gonna be there."

"Yeah." Sangster breathed a heavy sigh and clicked his tongue lightly. "Look, when you get the time, you can figure it out *with* them. But now is not the time."

"Yeah, okay." Alex nodded reluctantly.

He went back to his seat in front of Astrid, slumping. He heard her flipping pages as he fished out his phone and stared at it in frustration. Astrid tapped him on the shoulder.

Alex didn't respond. He was thinking about Minhi and Paul and Sid, and the last thing he wanted to deal with was Astrid, who had really come out of nowhere and within a day thrown his life upside down.

She tapped his shoulder again and cleared her throat.

"Yeah," he mumbled.

"You want to come sit with me?"

Why? He was whining inside his head. Alex looked back at her. "What's up?"

"I want to show you this."

Alex reluctantly got up and settled into the seat next to Astrid. "What do you got?"

"There are so many layers to this painting." Astrid sounded excited. "I can't believe I wasn't familiar with it. Minhi has a mind like a trap."

"I'll say." Alex changed the subject. "So, what is it we hope to accomplish by looking at the actual painting that we can't tell from an art book?"

"Well, for one thing, we can get a look at the physical paint and see if Bruegel left anything in it that they didn't pick up. That's more of a Polidorium activity. But for another—Alex, Bruegel actually touched this painting. There might be a spiritual spell I can do to learn about what he was thinking when he made it."

"More of your magic beans?" It didn't sound all that special to call yourself a witch if your power basically amounted to using premade tools.

She studied his face. "You don't think much of Prepared Spells, do you?"

"I don't know what to think." Alex shook his head. "It's really not my . . . I'd say *concern*, but that sounds so formal."

"You think it's . . . a cheat? I'm using someone else's work?"

He was actually thinking, *I just found out my mother is a witch, and she was able to shut a window with a few words. She didn't need to throw any prepared weapon at it.*

She closed the book and set her hands on it, crossing them. "Do you know how we prepare them?" When Alex shook his head, she continued. "We make them ourselves. There are some spells that can be done on the fly, with a flurry of words, but many of them take more incantation than you're likely to have time for in the field. Remember also that spells of conflict are especially costly and take more time and energy. So we very caringly prepare spells. It takes me hours and weeks to put a full library together. Everyone prepares them for themselves. The decoding spell you saw me use, I made myself."

"I've . . . seen other spells cast," Alex said. "And they didn't use tools."

Astrid nodded. "This would be your mother."

Alex's ears pricked up. "Yes."

Astrid seemed to brighten when the subject came up. "Amanda is very much admired in the community. I mean, people talk about her, Alex. She can work faster and more efficiently than anyone of her generation and many older witches. She has both the innate talent and the years of training." Astrid paused and leaned forward, looking the way Sid often did when he learned something new about vampires. "Can you *tell* me about her? What was it like growing up with such a powerful witch?"

Alex felt his mouth drop open as he searched for an answer. The truth was going to be embarrassing. She seemed to know more about his mother than he did. "Um, she didn't ever use her power when I was around."

Astrid didn't seem to understand this. "Really?"

"Really," Alex said. "I didn't know." It was worse than that; he didn't just not know—his parents had actively hidden the existence of the paranormal world from him. Vampires, werewolves, and witches, ghosts and zombies, and of course any significance to Alex Van Helsing's name were all the imaginary stuff of books and movies. His parents had lied about the fact that the books, especially, carried clues regarding the truth about all of those things. He wanted to say, *What else can you tell me about my mother?* but he felt himself brimming with irritation.

"She must have sacrificed a great deal," Astrid said.

Must have sacrificed. For Dad first, then for Alex and his fraternal twin, Judith, then for his three younger sisters. For all of them.

But what did that mean, *must have sacrificed*? Was Astrid suggesting Mom was miserable? *No, no, stop flying off the handle.* He caught himself overreacting. He slowed down the way his father had taught him, as he would if he suddenly found himself losing his balance on a ski slope. He was hearing every word that Astrid said and for some reason he was giving it all the worst possible reading. Why was he doing that? It didn't matter. *This panic you're feeling is not real.*

Alex shrugged. "I really couldn't say."

Astrid's eyes darted rapidly and she seemed to be looking over his eyebrows, and if he didn't know better he'd think she was trying to read his mind. Could witches do that? "There's a lot going on in there."

"Can I ask you a question?" Alex asked.

"Anything!" she said. "Alex, do you know you're the only teenager I've met who's aware of this weird little world we run in? It's *nice* not to have to pretend to be normal. Go ahead, ask away."

"When you said that you insisted on working with a Van Helsing—I guess I'm confused. My mom was the witch, but what's so special about the Van Helsings?"

She shook her head and smiled. "Alex, you should know this stuff."

"Yeah, I'm getting that."

"Let's just say that just because your dad says the family belongs on the Polidori side of the equation doesn't make it necessarily so."

"What do you mean? We're not magic users."

"Well, *you* are, aren't you?"

"I have a . . ." He looked at his hands as though he had the right description written on his palm. "I have an ability to sense evil. I can't do spells or anything. And apparently it's unusual."

"And you're thinking you inherited this from your mom?"

Alex shrugged.

"Well." Astrid leaned forward conspiratorially. "I do know something about this. You're *not* the first Van

Helsing to have power when it comes to vampires. You might be the first in a long time, but not the first. The Van Helsing that John Polidori met and worked with is someone my people admire greatly."

"You mean Abraham?" Alex knew that she was talking about *the* Van Helsing, Alex's great-great-great-grandfather, who had given Bram Stoker notes on the hunt for Dracula that had played out in the 1880s. As a man in his twenties, Abraham had met John Polidori, who had started by faking his own death in 1821 and hunting Lord Byron. By the 1850s, Polidori was gathering vampire hunters and sharing information around the globe, starting a network of agents in the field and writers who were paid, coerced, recruited, and seduced into seeding information into literature. By the time of the *Dracula* affair at the end of the 1800s, Abraham was in his late seventies and John Polidori was long dead, finally actually dead. But what Alex had never understood was that Polidori and Van Helsing had coordinated their efforts on occasion with witches.

"Yes," Astrid said. "But even Abraham didn't have the power you have. The gift belonged to Abraham's first son before he died. That's the last one we know of."

What? This was all new information for Alex. There had been other Van Helsings with the abilities he was developing? He felt a rush of excitement and relief. "This is incredible," Alex said. "You know about my obscure uncles."

"We find you very interesting."

"Great! So what happened to my . . ." Alex tried to do the math. "Great-great-great-uncle?"

Astrid looked up as though reading through a file floating in the air. "Abraham failed to find anyone who could help him with the powers he was developing. The boy went insane and died in a mental institution in the 1870s."

Alex paused, then mumbled, "Oh."

Astrid quickly changed the subject. "So, do your friends know about you?" she asked. "Minhi seemed to get really serious when you started asking about the painting."

"Yeah." Alex nodded resignedly. "They do. I tell them pretty much everything."

"So you hate to say what's in your head but you talk a great deal." Astrid smiled.

"It's not like that." Alex brightened suddenly. "Sid is a genius when it comes to vampires. He catches things that the Polidorium can miss. Paul is a rock of support. I need him. And Minhi is . . ."

Astrid studied him, reminding him again of a curious

bird. "A mind like a trap."

"She's also a kung fu master," Alex added.

The young witch smiled. "You're very protective of them."

"I don't know if *protective* is the word, I—they took me in."

Astrid shook her head. "Alex, you have such a destiny," she said. "I don't think you realize it. And I just wouldn't want to see you throw it away."

Alex rose. "Look, don't take this the wrong way, but I don't know you. I've worked with Sangster and the Polidorium for months, and *they* trust you, so I'm following their lead. And I'm not trying to be hard on you. But it's not as easy for me to trust you. Minhi and Paul and Sid—they're like family to me, and I *do* trust them. So I have no idea what you mean when you say I'm throwing my life away, but listen: It's *my* life."

He turned abruptly and went to his seat, wrapping his jacket around him. He needed to sleep.

"Okay, but I think we should talk some more about Bruegel," she offered, ignoring his outburst.

He shook his head and closed his eyes. He couldn't do this right now. "Just get some sleep, Astrid."

CHAPTER 10

The Prado Museum in Madrid, a vast, light gray palace lined with columns and plants, well-manicured lawns, and trees, had three entrances. The first, Puerta de Goya Alta, was for tourists. The second, the Puerta de los Jerónimos, was for groups, and the third, Puerta de Murillo, was for reservations and guests. At six A.M. on Tuesday morning Alex found himself in Spain going in the third way. They had four hours before the museum opened.

Alex, Astrid, and Sangster left Armstrong reading in the Spanish-loaned van at the curb in front of the Atocha Metro stop and crossed the busy avenue in front of the museum at a run. As they neared the Puerta de

Murillo, Alex could hear morning birds calling in the trees, and he could see a man in a suit walking down the steps to meet them.

As they approached, Alex whispered to Sangster, "So they're actually going to let us look at it?"

"It's a favor from the government."

"Do you guys have agents in every government?"

"Not an agent, in this case," corrected Sangster. "A friend who owes us a favor."

"*Buenos dias,*" the man said as he approached. He was tall, with silver hair and glasses and a neat mustache. Alex had the vague sense that they'd seen him before. They stopped in the shadow of the columns before the Puerta de Murillo. "Come, come, we have not much time if you want to get a good look." The man gestured for them to follow. He led them up wide steps to a large wooden door that lay half open. "We have set aside space in the lower level, where the jewels are kept."

"Are you the curator?" Alex asked.

Sangster said, "Alex, this is Federico Cazorla, Minister of Foreign Affairs."

Alex shook the man's hand, and just as he was marveling that for some reason they were going to be led around by a minister, he lit on the man's name. "Cazorla?"

"Alex!" came another voice, and he looked ahead to see a girl just coming out the door. She was smoothing down a brown dress that perfectly complemented a familiar green scarf on her neck. Her brown hair was shoulder-length, wavy, and lush. It had grown since he had seen her last. The girl ran and nearly tackled him, throwing her arms around him and kissing each cheek.

"Vienna," Alex said, smiling. "I had no idea you were back in . . ."

"Back home? Of course." Her voice was husky and lush.

Alex turned to Astrid. "This is Vienna Cazorla; she used to be a student at Glenarvon-LaLaurie."

"Except that it wasn't originally called Glenarvon-LaLaurie. Just LaLaurie, until Alex blew up his own school and the students were thrown together." Vienna's huge eyes crinkled when she talked and held him momentarily spellbound. The scarf moved with her throat, and Alex remembered the scarf had once been alive, a magical curse that bound her to put Alex in harm's way as surely as it held her head to her shoulders. She was still wearing it, and he wondered if it still held her in thrall, or if she just loved scarves.

Astrid introduced herself and Vienna kissed the air next to each of Astrid's cheeks. She took Astrid and Alex by the arms and led them in, ignoring the adults. "Alex, I didn't know you would be bringing a friend."

"I gotta say, I didn't know I'd even be here!" Alex replied. "And now I can't believe *you're* here."

"I live here," she said cheerily. "How long are you in Madrid?"

"A day at most. The Polidorium has six days to stop the end of the world, I think," he said casually.

Vienna nodded. "So, you'll be staying at my pensione tonight. You won't begrudge a friend the opportunity to be hospitable. Will you?"

Alex smiled. He'd forgotten about Vienna, the arm-sweeping, flirty vivaciousness of her. They all looked back at Sangster.

Sangster shrugged. "I think that sounds swell."

"You hear that?" Alex asked, smirking. "Swell."

With that settled, they stepped into the museum, and Alex was immediately overwhelmed by the expansiveness of the place—just the first hall was massive, with long red-and-gold carpeting and vaulted ceilings, and paintings stretching back as far as the eye could see. All was deserted other than a small army of custodians wearing blue overalls, walking mopping buckets and sweeping with wide cloth brooms.

"This is the jewel of *la ciudad*." Vienna slowed them

expertly as Minister Cazorla pulled ahead. "*El Prado* houses over 7,600 paintings, over a thousand sculptures, and several thousand more works of art of various kinds. Most are in storage, but nearly two thousand works are on display. It is the largest art museum in the entire world."

"You are *really* enjoying this," Alex said.

"*Por supuesto,* I am just getting star—" Vienna looked up as an alarm suddenly rang out.

"What's that?" Alex asked.

"Someone broke a laser alarm," said the minister, and they all started to run. Alex watched as red lights began to flash, and he heard heavy locks clicking shut on doors as they moved closer to a stairwell.

As they covered the eighth of a mile or so until they reached the second-floor wing that housed the Bruegel, Alex heard voices. Security guards in black suits emerged from nowhere and pushed past them, and by the time they reached *The Triumph of Death*, there was a crowd of about twenty.

The minister called out to a bald man in a black suit, "Tomás, *que tal?*"

"That's your curator," Sangster said, as Tomás looked them over and then back at the painting.

The curator said, "*No se, pero alguien la toco.*"

"He says someone touched the painting," Vienna offered. Alex slipped out of her grasp and edged around the crowd to get his first look at *The Triumph of Death*.

The painting was five feet wide and four feet tall, in a massive wooden frame, and lit up by aimed track lighting. Alex looked down the wall past a hundred other works to see small red lights, lasers that would sense if someone got within inches of the canvas.

"Did they damage it?" Alex asked.

Vienna shook her head. "It does not look like it."

Alex looked at Sangster. "Why would someone mess with the same painting we were coming to look at?"

"Yeah, I'm wondering the exact same thing," Sangster said.

Tomás was in a fury, questioning the guards. He called over a custodian, who entered from the far hall, and interrogated him. The custodian, about twenty, handsome and green-eyed, looked profoundly shocked. Alex gathered that he hadn't seen anything. Tomás turned back to the minister and started speaking rapidly in Spanish.

"Uh-oh," Sangster said.

"What?"

Vienna whispered huskily, "The curator is worried, and he doesn't want us to remove it and look at it. It all seems strange now."

"Tell him it's important."

Vienna frowned at Alex. Like that was gonna happen. "How would you say it? Papa has got this."

Minister Cazorla spoke with ease now, using a soothing but firm tone. Alex got the gist of what he was saying: this is important; these people are here on an assignment, and the painting is untouched, and anyway we have a chance to look at it.

While the minister was explaining the situation, Alex looked back at the painting. As he moved closer, he caught a flicker of light off the painting's surface. He stepped to the side, looking at it as it hung there. The flicker was odd, not covering the whole painting. "Huh."

Sangster heard him. "What?"

"I don't know. Something isn't ri—"

Alex took a moment to take in the whole room. The custodian caught his eye again, moving around the corner with his mop and broom. Among the cleaning fluids and utilitarian white canisters in his bucket Alex saw a shiny brown can. It caught his eye because it didn't fit; it looked—grocery-store-bought, not like something a custodian would clean a museum with.

He began moving toward the custodian slowly to get a better look.

For a moment he saw the image on the spray can. It was a picture of a man with a model head of thick brown hair. It was hair spray. Spraying that on a painting would leave a shiny film.

They were just at the corner and Alex called, "Excuse me."

The custodian looked back. "*Que? Lo siento, no . . .*"

"Is that hair spray?" Alex made a motion of spraying his head as he walked closer to the man.

Without another word, the custodian slung the bucket at Alex and it clattered toward him, barely missing him.

The custodian turned and ran, his hat flying off as he really started to move. He was still carrying the mop. It was clearly meant to be used as a weapon. *Who are you?* Alex thought. *You're not a vampire and you're not one of us, so who are you?*

The blond custodian reached an exit door to a stairwell and slid to a stop next to it. He looked back at Alex as he slipped something out of his pocket. Alex felt adrenaline flood through his chest.

Don't let it take you. What's going on?

He's got something in his hand. It's a—

It looked like a deck of cards. The custodian took less than a second to swipe it across the magnetic sensor next to the door and the door opened. Of course. Because the door had been locked by the alarm, and this guy was prepared to unlock it. But if he wasn't stealing, what was he doing?

Alex heard the others running behind him with the alarms still blaring. The man got through the door, and Alex moved fast to get in behind him. In the stairwell, the man ran up the first flight of stairs and started to turn as Alex took off after him. The door closed, and Alex suddenly heard pounding on the metal exterior as the others reached it, unable to pass.

"Hey! Stop! Who are you?" Alex cried.

The custodian turned at the first landing and swept around with the mop, catching Alex in the chest. Alex felt the air rush from his lungs as the mop bashed him back against the wall. The man let the mop drop as Alex kicked it aside and jumped, grabbing for the man's ankles.

The man went down silently, already rolling. He was an expert, and as he spun Alex's grasp weakened. He kicked up, smashing Alex in the ear as he went.

Within seconds, they were up again and running. They covered three flights before Alex heard the first-floor door opening down below, the security guards finally producing their own key cards.

The man reached the top of the stairs, swiped his card at a door, and pushed, running. Alex went after him, this time barely catching the door as it started to close.

They were on the roof of the main hall of the Prado Museum. Chill morning air swept over the gravel as Alex picked up speed.

"What are you doing? Who are you?" Alex called again. *I can run just as fast as you can.* He didn't have a go package with him or he would have seriously considered shooting the guy with a wooden bolt. But that didn't seem right. Alex did have climbing gear in the tear-away lining of his jacket; maybe he could just grapple the guy. But no, that might injure the stranger's neck or something, and murder was not on Alex's list of ambitions. Vampires were dead already and didn't count, but this man was definitely human.

They rounded a rooftop utility building, and Alex took in the breadth of Retiro Park beyond the building, a carpet of trees with a huge pond, just across the lawn of the museum.

And there was a flat, colorful object flapping next to the edge of the roof. It was hard to recognize until the guy stopped next to it and began to reach down. *No way.*

The custodian crouched for a moment, grabbed a long, curved aluminum tube, and lifted it. An entire hang glider, thirteen feet across, swept up around him.

"Oh, *come on!*" Alex shouted as he tried to close the distance.

The custodian looked back wordlessly and leapt. For a moment he began to fall, and then Alex watched from the edge of the building as the glider caught the air, taking the custodian out over the lawns, swooping up and disappearing behind the trees of Retiro Park.

Alex put his hands on his knees. *You have got to be kidding.* "It's not that easy, Quiet Man." He could run back down the stairs, but the doors were liable to give him trouble. Alex studied his surroundings, feeling each second of indecision tick away his chances of catching the stranger.

They were four stories up, and the wall was slick stone, leading down at intervals to french doors with small balconies. Perhaps he could climb down. But it would take too much time.

No, no. He looked out across the lawn and saw a light pole about thirty yards away. He reached into his Polidorium-issued jacket and pulled back a Velcro flap, producing a small hand-held grappling gun. It had a miniature hook and an air tube, but he wasn't sure if it would reach far enough.

He brought up the grappling hook and aimed at one

of the arms of the light pole.

"It won't reach," Sangster said, running up behind him. Alex heard the rest of them coming now, too. "That's fifty feet at least and that thing won't shoot past thirty—plus there's gravity."

Alex lowered his arm, consciously willing the surge of adrenaline to drain away. "Who the heck was *that*?"

"I don't know," Sangster said. "But he left a message."

CHAPTER 11

"They will allow us one hour with the painting," Sangster said as they stepped through a heavy metal door and into a vault of stone and steel. Alex found Astrid and Vienna standing next to glass cases displaying more jewels than he had ever seen. "This is the jewel collection of the Grand Dauphin Louis, son of Felipe V," Sangster explained. "The vault is open to visitors during the day."

A white rolling table on wheels sat in the center of the room with a heavy wooden cover over it. It looked like a gurney. "Is that the painting?" asked Alex.

"Yes."

"What are we doing with it?"

"Scanning it."

"Hasn't it been scanned?" Alex said. "It's in every art book we've looked at."

"This is not your ordinary scanner," Sangster replied.

Tomás the curator and Minister Cazorla conferred for a moment, and then Tomás turned to an electronic keypad on the wall at a second door in the back. A glass case of rubies, diamonds, and gold swung open slowly to reveal a circular metal door seven feet high. The curator tapped a long code into another keypad, and then Alex heard a series of heavy clicking sounds buried deep in metal.

With a pneumatic hiss the second door opened inward, swinging wide to reveal a vault. Sangster and Cazorla held either end of the gurney and lifted it over the lip of the door.

The room within was sterile and cold, and in the center stood a tall frame that looked like an airport metal detector. The frame itself had four spindly metal arms half folded, hanging there like the door expected to defend itself. Tomás looked back at the gurney and pressed a button on the inside of the frame. The frame widened slowly, sliding along tracks in the ground, until Tomás seemed satisfied it was wide enough.

He nodded to the two men and they rolled the gurney the rest of the way, stopped it at the edge of the frame, and slowly removed the wooden cover. Now the five-foot-wide painting lay between the metal posts, naked on the table.

When Tomás touched a button on the side, Alex heard a churning sound and watched as the painting lifted slowly off the table, borne by countless tiny Plexiglas posts, until the painting seemed to float a half inch off the tabletop.

"You're making a 3-D image of the painting."

Sangster nodded at Alex's guess as the robot arms unfolded and began to sweep slowly back and forth, all the way down the table and back up and over, again and again, streams of red laser light faintly visible from the glowing edges of the arms. The arms crawled like a spider over the painting as the frame slowly moved along its tracks.

"We need to know everything," Sangster said. "What might be painted under it and what might be hidden in it. This is the best way we have of capturing the entire painting." He turned and pointed to a display screen on the wall behind the frame, which was now showing the entire *Triumph of Death* at twice its normal size. Alex was once again filled with horror by the images of the people with their mouths open, screaming. But this time he could see the countless brushstrokes.

Alex saw a shimmer coming from the painting again.

"You said the guy left a message."

Sangster nodded and asked Cazorla something, who turned to Tomás. The curator spoke and Cazorla translated as he directed their attention to the screen.

"This is the painting. We can display different layers of it already. We're just getting more details now." The image shifted, and the entire painting seemed to lift toward them and away, revealing white and gray pencil strokes underneath. "These are the original pencil drawings underneath, the guides that Señor Bruegel used."

Now the layer of colors and brushstrokes lowered back over the pencil marks and seemed to recede. A new image came into view in the lower right corner, looking like spray paint on the screen—the mark left by the custodian, a simple X. Tomás fiddled with the controls to sharpen the image. "This is this morning's addition to the work," Cazorla said, sounding annoyed.

"We saw it the moment your man ran," Sangster told Alex.

"X marks the spot?"

"We'll be able to remove it, *gracias a dios*," Cazorla said. "It is a very mild hair spray."

Alex looked at Sangster. "I don't get what this is about. The custodian was not one of the Scholomance. Not Hexen. And he wasn't an amateur. And he left this just as we got here. So what is the message?"

"We're not sure, but he was careful not to damage the painting," Sangster said.

Tomás suddenly let out an agitated curse.

The curator waved a hand, looking at a computer screen nearby, and then sent the image to the main screen.

The camera zoomed in again on the corner of the painting below the X, and the X lifted away as the curator dismissed that layer. Now Alex saw two human figures, a man and a woman singing as a skeleton crept up behind them. "*No es azul,*" Tomás said in what sounded like shock.

"It's not blue," Vienna translated from over by the wall.

"What does that mean?" Alex asked.

Tomás spoke rapidly in Spanish, and Cazorla said, "He says there's a layer of paint, very thin, on the woman's dress. It's—you see, it has always been blue."

"And it is blue," Alex said, confused, looking at the woman, whose dress was indeed a blue-colored satin.

"But the blue is *new*," Minister Cazorla said. "Or, not *so* new, but newer than the painting."

Tomás shifted his hand in the air as if estimating and spoke while Vienna translated. "He says it's a modern pigment, probably less than fifty years old." The curator tapped a few buttons and, in the computer image on the screen, the layer of blue color on the dress lifted off and away.

The woman's dress was a sort of burnt red underneath.

They all stood staring. "So," Alex said, "someone changed the red dress to blue."

"Right," Cazorla answered. "That is stunning. This is an amazing discovery."

"But just so we're clear," Alex said, "this alteration that the custodian marked for us was probably done fifty years ago."

"Give or take."

A bell chimed and the sweeping arms retracted themselves and lay silent. Tomás was still enrapt at the image of the blue dress. But it didn't get them any closer to stopping the Triumph that the Queen had in mind.

"That's it," Sangster said. "We'll take the image and look at it. We need to go."

"Wait." Alex gestured toward Astrid. "She said maybe she could get something off it. Can she touch the painting?"

The curator and Minister Cazorla conferred briefly, and then Cazorla nodded to Sangster. "The corner flap only. Not on the surface of the painting."

Astrid nodded and asked them all to stand back. She approached the painting as though it were a patient in a hospital bed. For a long time she waited at the edge of it, her bare hand at her side, her fingers twitching.

Who was this girl? Why was she here?

Suddenly Astrid's hand shot out and she touched the edge and closed her eyes, the many peculiar pigtails in her hair quivering above her thin neck. She whispered, "An assignment. A secret contract to make a painting. The master painter, traveling in his peasant's hood, left in the middle of the night, disappeared to a place unknown to him, a castle of great black towers, somewhere far from home. His patrons told him what they wanted, showed him visions of the Triumph, and rewarded him well."

Astrid shook her head and then let go of the painting.

"So it's confirmed." Sangster nodded slowly. "The painting was to be a guide."

The team had a mystery now. They also had a confused curator eager to get everything back to normal.

Within half an hour, they were far from the arriving museum crowds, and at the palatial pensione of Vienna Cazorla.

CHAPTER 12

"At this time of day, there is nobody out." Vienna dragged Alex and Astrid to one of the sets of french doors in the living room of her pensione. She opened the doors, and they stepped out onto the balcony. Alex pulled his jacket a little tighter as the breeze blew in. The mid-morning was cold and gray, and below, a great square was empty except for a newsstand where an attendant rearranged magazines and helped himself to a Fresca from one of the refrigerator units.

Astrid looked around. "I thought these kinds of apartments—uh, pensiones—were usually hotels."

"This one was." Vienna nodded. "But when we moved from Seville, my mother fell in love with it."

The pensione that Vienna Cazorla shared with her parents took up two entire floors of an ancient building in the Chueca neighborhood in Madrid. Vienna's mother was traveling to visit her brother up north, leaving the place to just Vienna and her dad. It was a cavernous apartment of sculptures and fresh flowers, and Alex heard parrots talking somewhere. He had the sense he could get lost here.

Behind Alex, Sangster and Armstrong were turning Vienna's dining table into an op center. "Okay," Sangster called.

Alex turned to see that Sangster had found butcher paper and had laid it out across the table, while Armstrong had a few Polidorium computers plugged in and sitting to the side. The teacher was writing key words with a marker.

"Where did you find butcher paper?" Vienna asked.

"At the butcher's in the square." Sangster underlined the word CUSTODIAN. "Your dad pointed it out to me when he went back to work." He paused. "Okay. Let's talk about the janitor."

"Well, he shows up for one reason and one reason only," said Alex. "Doesn't want to fight, doesn't want to talk. All he does is put an X on the painting."

"Exactly marking a place where the painting has been altered," said Astrid.

"Is there something important about the woman in the blue dress?" Alex asked.

Armstrong was tapping away and stopped to scan an article on the painting. She held up a hand. "They've actually been written about. There's a poem—"

"Plath," Sangster said. "Sylvia Plath, yeah, it was a . . . that's right, she wrote a poem called "Two Views of a Cadaver Room" about the couple in the corner. She was impressed with them because they're blissfully unaware of their approaching death."

"It's a common thesis," Armstrong offered.

"Yeah, but what does it *mean*?" Alex wrung his hands. "Be of good cheer? Be blissfully unaware? Don't be blissfully unaware?"

"And, of course, there's the altered color itself," Astrid said. "From red, a color of passion, to blue, a color of . . . what? Cold? Death?"

"We don't need an alteration to remind us to think about death," Alex said. "It's called *The Triumph of Death*."

"No, the alteration has to be a pointer to something beyond the painting. Something we would miss otherwise. Someone made this alteration in the last fifty years and someone else marked it for us today. Whoever they are, they are leading us to something." Sangster sat down, running his fingers through his hair. "Everybody get reading. We'll break for lunch in an hour."

They dug into everything they could find on *The Triumph of Death*. Essays, articles, poems, tribute paintings by modern artists. Alex knew what they were doing—they were swimming through details deliberately, waiting for something to pop. Outside, Alex was aware of the ebb and flow of traffic, bursts of people followed by near-desertion of the streets. By noon the plaza below was filled with people.

Just as Alex felt his brain turning to Jell-O, he heard a knock at the door and Vienna ushered in a full meal, a paella of rice, scallops, chicken, and shrimp, with red wine for the agents. "Take a break," Sangster ordered.

Alex wolfed down his paella, suddenly aware of his hunger, as Astrid and Vienna chatted.

Astrid asked Vienna a thousand questions, drawing out the girl's history and her time at Glenarvon-LaLaurie and even a hint of her dark adventure with the vampires. When Vienna grew uncomfortable, Alex saw that Astrid expertly charmed her, touching her shoulder and turning her attention to the pensione. Vienna had a great deal of art of her own, but Alex recalled that Vienna was a writer—or at least had been producing manga with Minhi back at school before her sudden departure.

"What do you write now?" Astrid asked. They had

risen and wandered about the room, and Alex joined them.

"What does everyone write?" Vienna's eyes crinkled. "Some poetry. I'm trying to understand short stories but they're maddening. It's a curse that there are so many great Spanish short story writers to contend with."

Vienna stopped at the window, looking down at the flower vendors on the streets below. "The first time I found out about your strange double life," she said suddenly, cocking her head at Alex, "we were standing at a window like this."

Alex did remember. "Yeah, Elle was below, waiting." It seemed like a long time ago.

Vienna shivered. "I think we need a fire to warm things up in here."

At one stucco wall next to a case of crystal, a low fireplace sat with a redbrick stoop, the entire fire and chimney recessed behind the stucco. Vienna dropped primly onto a settee by the fireplace. She turned a gas key in the wall and a pilot light ignited a small stack of wood. She stoked the flames lightly.

Astrid looked up at a high-pitched cheeping sound from the chimney. "What is that?"

"Birds—chimney swifts." Vienna adjusted the logs on the fire. "They're dear little things."

Alex joined Vienna by the fire and rubbed his face.

"Your friend follows you everywhere," Vienna whispered. Alex looked back and saw that indeed Astrid had moved a few steps in his direction.

Alex glanced sideways at Vienna's scarf and whispered, "So how have you been? Is that thing still . . ."

Vienna's eyes reflected the fire, but she didn't look at him as she smiled. "Alive? Yes. But it no longer holds my head on."

"Well, that's a relief." Alex rubbed his hands before the fire. "I didn't get a chance to say good-bye. I'm sorry for what happened at the ball. I'm sorry our date got all . . . screwed up."

Vienna stood straighter and turned to him, leaning in closer. "We both know I was not the one you wanted to be going with."

The sound of cheeping chimney swifts above them grew and dropped rhythmically. Alex wondered how birds could comfortably live among the smoke. He shook his head. There wasn't time for this. They would be living among darkness and vampires soon. He looked back to Sangster. "We have *six days*. And now we're wondering about, what—"

Sangster summed it up. "A running conspiracy to alter a sixteenth-century Flemish painting in order to record clues about stopping the catastrophe the painting represents."

Alex shook his head in frustration. "But where does that leave *us*? Bruegel the painter is not connected to us. But the custodian, who is also not connected to us, is guiding us to clues about a catastrophe that a powerful sorceress could bring about. According to the spell Astrid did when she touched the painting, Bruegel was put up to painting it, paid by these black tower people. All of whom may be connected. Do you know what that means?" He rubbed his temple. Something was . . . something was . . .

He suddenly felt static. Alex looked around, then shook his head to clear it.

"Tell us," Sangster said.

"It means that someone has been planning all along to warn us but either can't or won't." He paused. "Wait." The static was there, hissing, the burbling of the birds seeming to grow and join the sound. "Do you hear that?"

Sangster scanned the room. "Yes."

A scuttling sound, clacking and scraping, grew in the walls themselves.

Flecks of soot began to fall in the fireplace. "Who knows we're here?"

Armstrong stood. "We ordered the paella in."

The static began to roar in Alex's head and he staggered. *Stop. Just listen to it. Don't let it overwhelm you.*

Astrid whispered something and then drew what looked like a shimmering green penlight from her coat. She flicked her hand and the thing telescoped, once and again, until it had grown out to the full glimmering green staff he had seen her wield before.

"What's that?" Vienna looked up as the sound of clacking and creaking echoed through the walls. The stucco in front of the chimney was cracking, bowing out, as if something were struggling to move down inside of it.

Alex heard a ratcheting sound and saw Sangster drawing a Beretta from a go package. Armstrong had one as well and they were backing up, scanning.

A heavy sound smacked into the glass of the french doors, and Alex saw something strike and glance away. He caught the shape of a bird's wings as it bounced and disappeared.

Bits of stucco began to crumble and fall from the chimney. Alex scrambled for the go package and grabbed a glass ball and a Polibow. He tried to feel the shape of the thing causing his brain to sizzle with static. "Sangster, I don't know what it is, but it's big."

Smoke and fire burst from the fireplace. Soot

exploded into the room and suddenly the whole apartment was a cloud. Alex felt more than saw Astrid step forward next to him, her staff raised.

"Everybody fan out so we don't shoot one another," Sangster shouted, a shadow in the plumes of soot, as high-pitched cheeping burbled and Alex saw its form slice past Sangster's head. He hissed in pain, grabbing his forehead.

Alex barely had time to see another bird, slick and narrow and cigar-shaped, dive out and fly right for his face. He put up his hand, brushing at it. *"Gyahh!"*

Glass crashed as a bird bashed into a lamp, and now the sound intensified, birds and more birds, three and then six and more, pouring into the room. Something sliced past Alex's ear and he felt a sharp sting and then blood trickling.

Alex spun and saw the creature, a gray bird that seemed to glow with streams of glistening red that enveloped it, swoop out of sight and then come back. It flew for his head, and he saw its open beak, a perversion of a tiny bird's. It grabbed his shoulder with its claws and started lapping at the blood on his ear.

He swatted it hard and sent it smacking into an end table, losing his footing. A pair of wineglasses burst as he started to fall, and he landed hard on his elbow, glass crunching through his sleeve.

The birds were everywhere.

"Alex!" Vienna called, and he saw her legs against the wall, and she was dropping to the ground. There was a bird at her neck, tugging at her scarf. "No, no, no!"

Alex scrambled up to the table, threw the glass ball he'd been holding, and watched it sail through the cloud and hit the wall above her, glass tinkling and water spraying.

The bird at Vienna's neck sizzled and dropped away, snarling with a roar most unbird-like as it turned in the air. Its eyes glowed red as it dove for Alex, tiny talons extended.

"Cleanse thee!" Astrid cried from out of the smoke, and her staff came flying, smacking the bird midflight. As she struck it, the thing burst into flame and flopped over Alex's head to land on the table.

There was a crackling sound as the butcher paper caught fire.

Alex coughed. "What *is* this?"

"Bloodwork," Sangster shouted. *Bloodwork.* That was vampire magic, altering living and dead things with enchanted blood. The most powerful could make almost anything with it.

A muffled chorus of cheeping grew, and there was a

burst of glass as the french doors gave way, and now a stream of chimney swifts swarmed in. "Hit the deck!" Armstrong ordered. "We've got to get out of here."

Alex lay on the floor and watched maybe twenty birds swarm, zipping through the room, in and out of the smoke. He could hear the birds bashing into cases.

A gun flash drew Alex's eye and he saw Armstrong, a shadow in the soot, on her stomach, shooting several birds at the doorway, the brief light of her gun followed by the bursts of the creatures. They fell like little firebombs onto the floor. "They're blocking the door!" Armstrong called.

"Astrid, how many of those magic, uh, cleanse shots do you carry?"

"It's not a *shot*; I have to *hit* them to cleanse them." Astrid cried out a few feet away as one bird cheeped madly and yanked at one of the ponytails on her head.

Alex coughed and blinked for an instant, seeing bright streaks of light against his eyelids. He opened his eyes, wincing with pain. His contacts were beginning to swim with the soot. The smoke had grown even darker, impenetrable.

Wait, go back, he told himself. He held his eyes closed and forced away the sounds of grunting and cursing and the bashing of glass and wood, filling his mind with static. With his eyes open, the static was just static, but closed, he could see it take shape, and he watched twenty streaks of red light zip across the black underside of his eyelids.

"Stop shooting, you're going to hit someone!" He held out his hand, groping in the darkness. "Astrid, take my hand."

Alex heard her crawl beside him and then she had his hand. Astrid's was cold and small, and the static seemed to dissipate as she drew near. But the streaks were still there.

"I have to keep my eyes closed." He grabbed her whole arm. "We're getting up."

They rose and Alex got behind her, his chest against the bird-like bones of Astrid's back, holding her hand and her staff. "Okay, move with me."

"What?"

"Just . . . trust me, and cleanse." Soot slid down Alex's cheek as he put his face next to her. "Move with me."

Alex brought Astrid's arm up and felt her body uncoiling as she stretched, but she was stiff. "Let me lead." He saw a streak coming in fast. She seemed to relax and he began to spin, her leg following his.

"Here!" They swept their arms together, and Alex heard her utter the word *cleanse* as the staff touched the arc of light just as it reached them.

"Cleanse," they said together, another step, their arms coming up, a streak coming in fast against his closed eyes. Another burst of flame. "Cleanse," and another, and another, and another.

He could hear in the background holy water bursting in the fireplace as Sangster destroyed a handful of the creatures, and Armstrong was at the door, shooting at those that were swirling around there. Alex and Astrid concentrated on the streaks, Astrid swinging her staff as he guided her.

Finally they were still and there was a tiny cheep. Vienna gasped somewhere, and Alex saw a bird streaking, and he and Astrid swept toward it. *Burst.*

In the inky smoke, Sangster clapped out the fire on the table, and Alex felt everyone start to relax. Armstrong threw open the door and smoke began to pour out.

"Come on!" she coughed.

He opened his eyes and stopped, suddenly collapsing into a coughing fit. Astrid dropped next to him and grabbed his hand. "Come on."

They ran down the stairs as the sound of fire engines filled the air.

On the front stoop of the building, Vienna hugged Alex as Sangster spoke rapidly into a Bluetooth device. Astrid stood by herself, watching them.

"Clearly the Queen's people are watching us," Sangster

said as he got off the phone. "We need to get out of the street."

Vienna watched in horror as firemen arrived and ran in and out of her building, and all the residents of the lower floors gathered and watched. "I need to go up there."

Alex shook his head. "Don't. Not yet. It's not a fire anymore—it's just a lot of smoke. We have to think of what you're going to say."

"Oh, who cares what I *say*?" Vienna said. "It's what I *know*. My father will come back tonight, and he'll see that it's true."

"What?"

"That no matter how much you people have helped me, I'm cursed."

"You're not cursed. Well, you might be cursed with the wrong friends." Alex sighed, looking at Sangster and Astrid. "The Scholomance tried to kill us. Why didn't they just come in themselves?"

"It was dusk," Sangster said. "Most likely this was safer. Blood-magic-augmented birds. So we know the Scholomance is onto us, in Madrid looking for clues about the Triumph."

"Just like the guy at the Prado was onto us." Alex turned back to Vienna. "Listen, I think they wanted *us*, and when we're gone they won't be interested in you." He said this more because he desperately hoped it was true, not because he had any actual idea.

Alex paused, stood back, and looked around him, silently watching the firemen gathering and scratching their heads. The square near Vienna's building was crowded, and the coffee and pastry vendors casually moved their stands closer to the building, scavenging for more customers.

What am I doing? Alex found himself asking this again as he had done in the past. Was this his life now? Completely truant from school, off the grid as far as his parents were concerned, and doing life-or-death research in Spain? Getting his friends nearly killed—was there any friend he was going to have whom he wasn't going to put in danger?

He shook his head, bringing himself back to the present. *No, no. Get in the game.* "The Scholomance knew we were at the Prado. They're not stupid; they knew that we'd be looking into *The Triumph of Death.* But the rest—the altered colors on the lady's dress in the painting, does the Scholomance know about that?"

"I'm still going with no. The custodian and the color alterers are on our side, in a funny way. There's no reason to think the vampires would be clued into that."

"Assuming you're right," Alex said, "there could be more."

"More Scholomance vampires?" Sangster said. "You bet."

"No, more Strangers," Alex said. "This morning a man broke into the Prado just to point us in the right way to this painting. There is a conspiracy that the Polidorium has completely overlooked, that started at least as far back as Bruegel's visit to this . . . castle of black towers. And that conspiracy knows what you people—what we—are doing." He pointed at Sangster and Armstrong. "The Scholomance is following us, and there's a conspiracy that knows what's going on better than *we* do. But they *don't get involved*."

"Maybe they're a rogue element *inside* the Polidorium," Astrid said.

Sangster shook his head. "I can totally accept the theory of a rogue element that split off to place clues—but a rogue element that told Bruegel what to paint? That would predate the Polidorium by two hundred years."

Alex peered down the mental chessboard. The game was all off-kilter now. There were three players. "The vampires put a virus in the Polidorium database to throw us off the trail. And someone else is trying to get us back on track. That supports the theory that they're friends, at least. Whoever this conspiracy of Strangers is, they're on our side, not the Queen's. But they are not talking, and they sure weren't about to help us survive that attack."

Armstrong gave it a shot. "Maybe it's dangerous for them."

"I don't accept that," Alex said. "The Triumph of Death is dangerous for everybody."

"So they want to help but don't want to force us to the conclusions." Sangster shifted his weight.

Alex was looking at his watch. "The Dimmer Switch curse, the Triumph of Death, is a tool for sorcerers. And it's being used by Claire Clairmont to fulfill a destiny. And we don't know what's going through her mind." He shook his head in frustration. "I'm *sick* of being in the dark."

"We're all working on it, Alex," Sangster said evenly.

"Well, you have your experts; I have a few of my own," Alex said. He knew exactly who would be able to work through this stuff. He should have included them from the start. "I'm going back to school. There are some people I'd like to talk to."

CHAPTER 13

It was four o'clock in the morning by the time Alex stashed the Ninja motorcycle in the woods across from Glenarvon-LaLaurie. A bitter cold wind off Lake Geneva shot through him as he jogged out of the woods and across the street into the courtyard of the school, and as the front of the building came into view he saw a light on. In the second-floor drawing room that served as a small study, he could see silhouettes moving around. The hulking shadow of Paul turned to the window, and Alex waved quickly as he headed up the steps and inside.

"Oh, look, he's not dead yet," said Paul when Alex opened the door to the study hall.

Alex grimaced, letting his go package slide off his

arm and to the floor next to the door. He froze for a second, looking at Paul, Sid, and Minhi. They were all wearing jeans and sweatshirts, whatever they could throw on after he'd texted them in the middle of the night from the airplane. Paul was standing next to the window as if on guard while Sid fiddled with the old-fashioned fireplace, trying to get the wad of kindling started. Minhi was sitting at a heavy wooden cherry-red table with a stack of books opened and splayed out. She was picking up a large green thermos, but as he entered she put it down and rose, coming to hug him.

Sid stood up, brushing soot off his hands. "You are toast," he said after shaking Alex's hand. "I mean *toast*. Otranto is going to run you up a flagpole if you're not back today."

Alex raised his hands. "I've been gone a day and a half. Hang on, I'm just gonna shut the door." Alex looked out into the hall, which was empty. The only people awake in the building were likely to be kitchen staff getting ready for the morning. He closed the door and then turned back to them. "Did he call my parents?"

"Of course not," Paul said, leaning on the table. "Sid and I covered for you. We said you were sick in bed. But he's suspicious; he said he'd better see you come down today."

Minhi pointed at Paul and Sid as she scolded Alex. "You do realize that they're lying for you without even knowing why. They could get in serious trouble."

Alex nodded. Okay, that was true. "I totally did not ask anyone to do that," he said, but he knew that was not the way to treat a friend.

Minhi shook her head. "Where have you *been*?" she demanded. "You completely disappeared; we might have thought you were *dead*."

"Madrid," Alex said.

"You were in Spain?" Sid sat down and threw his sneakered feet up on the table. "For a day?"

Paul snickered. "You get any paella?"

"Yeah, Vienna ordered some in."

"You saw Vienna?" Minhi asked. Her mind seemed to trip through several options and suddenly she brought her hand to her throat and said, "Does she still have the . . ."

"Yeah, but she says it's not holding her head on anymore."

"You ask her to prove it or did you just take her word for it?" Paul asked.

"Totally learned my lesson on this." Alex held up his hands.

"Wait, wait, back up," Sid said, with a delirious sort of

smile on his face. "Why were you in Spain eating paella with Vienna?"

"Right," Alex said, suddenly trying to decide where to start.

"Why don't you start with, 'I suppose you're wondering why I've called you all here,'" said Minhi.

"Seriously?" Alex squinted.

Sid nodded. "Yeah, actually that would be very cool."

Alex smiled. "Okay, let me start with this: I'm really sorry, guys. I shouldn't have disappeared. There's something terrible going on. We're not really sure how to stop it. And I seem to be in a life now where the Polidorium snaps its fingers and I cross continents for them."

"So, what is it, Alex?" Minhi asked, her tone softening slightly. She had leaned back on the table next to Paul.

"Actually it is what you said: the Triumph of Death. Apparently the painting is an illustration of what the world will be like after Queen Claire sets off a curse. She will plunge the world into darkness, and the vampires will be free to run wild."

Paul exhaled. "So . . . how long do you have?"

"Till Monday, it looks like."

"Are you mad?" Paul said. "The world goes dark in less than a week?"

"Should we call home?" Minhi asked. "My mother

could warn the government in Mumbai."

"My dad might get home," Sid said, his eyes darting. "He's off consulting on something in Italy, I think. But he could get back to Canada. Everyone would need to get home."

Paul seemed to be thinking and then he deferred to Alex. "But you don't think that's a good idea."

Alex shrugged. "What would you say? 'Hi, Mom, my friend the vampire-hunting spy wants you to know that there might be a global catastrophe next week?' Without proof?"

"Right." Paul nodded. "So that's not the plan. But what is the plan?"

"We have to solve it." Sid rose and went to a whiteboard, and the other two instantly seemed to snap into a different mode, going around to take seats and pop open laptops. From the whiteboard Sid said, "What do we know?"

Without hesitation, Alex began to pour out the facts and soon the whiteboard filled with key words, *CLAIRE* and *TRIUMPH OF DEATH* and *STRANGERS* and *HEXEN.*

All horrible, all awful, of course, but even so, a wave of relief washed over Alex because he was sharing it with them. They were his team. As sure as Armstrong was Sangster's partner, he needed Paul, Sid, and Minhi to feel less alone and to think.

"Hexen?" Minhi raised a hand. "I don't recognize that."

"Ah. Right," Alex said. "That's a whole other organization, made up of witches."

"Wait. Astrid is one of them, isn't she?" Minhi guessed this before any evidence had been laid before her. "That's why she just turned up when Claire did. And so . . . that's why she's been missing, too."

"Yes. Did you happen to cover for her?"

Minhi shook her head. "No—maybe if you'd *asked*. Maybe if you'd said, 'Hey, Astrid and I are hopping over to Spain to see if Vienna can order us some paella.'"

"I totally did not know Astrid was involved," Alex said. "But she was here to investigate Claire."

"Claire," Sid said. "*There's* a nightmare."

Alex turned his chair and rested his hands on the back, looking at Sid. "You told us some stuff about Claire when Icemaker was here," he said. "Can you bring me up to speed?"

Sid leaned back and seemed to flip through pages in his mind. The boy was an encyclopedia of knowledge on vampires and everything related to them, and the group of vampires that circled around Lake Geneva was a favorite topic. "Well, we all know that she was the queen that Byron, or Icemaker, was trying to raise when he came back. But at first, Claire Clairmont was just a young woman who followed Lord Byron here from England with Mary Shelley and John Polidori. And Byron was cruelest with her—they had a baby, Allegra, who Byron took with him even when he turned his back on Claire. And then he got sick of taking care of the baby and had her put in a convent."

"Did Claire ever get to see either of them again?"

"No, and she was . . . enraged. But there was nothing she could do. And then she got word that Allegra had died without even hearing from her father. The girl died among strangers and was buried without Claire ever getting to see her again."

"But we know that Icemaker went through an awful lot to bring Claire back to life to rule as his queen," Alex said. "Why would that be? If he hated her so much."

Minhi glanced at Alex. "Sometimes we're obsessed with things we shouldn't be. Maybe his hatred of her turned into a kind of obsessive love."

"And he was a vampire," Alex said. "His empathy centers are all damaged, and obsession is what you get instead of love. So: we've got Icemaker, obsessed with Claire and bringing her back—and he's now safely locked away. And we've got Claire, obsessed with Ice-maker as far as we know, but also hating him. And now she's trying to set off the Triumph of Death."

"What did Claire's warning say? What is lost will be found? And you said this spell would give her command over the dead. She's lost Byron, but she also lost Allegra, her daughter," said Sid.

Minhi said, "If she encases the world in darkness, maybe she can bring her daughter back."

"Look, I feel as sorry for this lady as anybody. But sometimes we don't get what we want." Alex looked back at Minhi. "Sometimes we want something and the time for it just . . . passes. The thing we have to worry about now is how to stop it."

"You'll figure it out," Minhi offered.

"I'm worried we'll be too slow. We don't have the tools. It's like we're being played. The custodian at the Prado knew something, but he's part of the big con-spiracy of not talking, the rogue element, the Strangers. Screw that. They're playing with us, and we need to stop playing."

Alex's phone buzzed and he looked at it, then stepped to the window.

Down at the edge of the courtyard, Astrid was waiting on her Hexen motorcycle. Minhi and Paul looked over Alex's shoulder.

"You want to ask her in?" Paul said.

Alex shook his head. "I gotta go. There's one more person who should know what the clues mean and can tell us how to stop the Triumph of Death," Alex said. "We need to get the answers from him."

"Alex," Sid said, still at the table. "I know what you're thinking and it's crazy. 'Too dangerous' doesn't even begin to describe it."

"What?" Paul and Minhi asked at the same time.

Alex looked back at Sid. "He's the only one who will know how to deal with her."

Minhi asked, "Who?"

"Icemaker," said Alex. "I need to talk to Lord Byron."

CHAPTER 14

They called it Icemaker Station.

Very near the house on the shores of Lake Geneva where he had almost ended Alex Van Helsing's life, the immortal vampire once known as Lord Byron and code-named Icemaker waited and slept in a chunk of ice. The curse that Byron had taken on himself near the end of his mortal life, the magic that enabled him to use and freeze the liquid in the air around him, had provided a final retreat when the Polidorium had caught up with him and doused him with liquid nitrogen, one of the coldest substances on earth. Byron opted to continue the process and encase himself in a protective chunk of ice, and there he stayed.

His captors didn't take him very far. The seven-foot-tall, four-foot-wide chunk of ice that held Lord Byron rested in silence in a liquid-helium-cooled refrigerator the size of a small house securely reinforced in a cell built just for him, half a mile below Lausanne, Switzerland. Manned twenty-four hours a day by chemists and security guards, with extra chambers and cells both under construction and ready for future prisoners, Icemaker Station occupied three city blocks' worth of space below the Olympic Museum, an access point chosen in part for its outward serenity and its complete lack of connection to either the world of anti-vampirism or the world of ultra-low-temperature experimentation. The fact that there were five world-class high magnetic field laboratories around Lake Geneva, providing a rich source of new hires to work on Icemaker Station, was a bonus.

Within seven hours of leaving Vienna Cazorla behind, Alex was getting out of a van at the edge of Lake Geneva at the Olympic Museum, a severe white-stone building set off by a much more inviting park. As Alex ran up the granite steps in a leather jacket that did nothing to stop the leaching cold coming off the lake, he took in a whole garden of sculpture dedicated to the constant search for human physical perfection.

"Every cell in my body is telling me this is a bad idea, so pay close attention." Sangster was rattling off instructions as they walked. "Do everything the staff tells you. If a rule sounds stupid, do it anyway. Polidorium Incarceration are the most competent jailers on the face of the earth, so respect every word they say."

"I got it," Alex said, freezing.

"Astrid?" Sangster said.

She nodded. "Sure."

Fir trees and rich green shrubbery nestled against the cold and blinding-white concrete museum. Around it, Alex saw huge gray figures that held aloft the Olympic circles and cyclists arrested forever in bronze and, of course, the Olympic torch. When he beheld a gray sculpture of a pistol with its barrel twisted into uselessness by the Olympic Spirit, Alex briefly envisioned the Olympic Spirit as some shot-putting Jolly Green Giant, thundering across the countryside, throwing train cars and spitefully knotting the barrels of perfectly good gun sculptures.

This was the kind of place where, as a young man of certain expectations sent overseas, Alex was *supposed* to be spending his time. If he were to call his mom right now and tell her that he was visiting Le Parc Olympique, Lausanne, she would think that he had finally become the student she'd always wanted him to be. Extra points maybe if he said he was with the new girl from the Netherlands.

As Alex, Astrid, and Sangster walked swiftly through the glass doors and into the sweeping rotunda of the museum, where twenty-foot-tall wall screens ran constant loops of human victory, his heart sank.

They walked past the screens to a stairwell, to a staff elevator only Sangster could unlock.

"Here we go, then," Sangster said, and they plunged liked stones into the secret world they had chosen.

The door of the elevator opened, and they stepped into a stark white hallway where a Polidorium security guard examined Sangster's credentials before they could move on. Sangster was putting away the security card he carried in his wallet when they heard the approach of heavy heels smacking against tile.

All three turned around to see a tall woman with tightly curled short hair, wearing a white coat, approaching, swinging her arms like an automaton. "Agent Sangster, we're almost ready for you," she said. "You're early. I don't remember you ever being early for anything."

Sangster's mouth curled only slightly into a smile, and it might actually have been more of a grimace. "Alex,

Astrid, this is Dr. Bella Kristatos. She's our director of cryogenics and altered states."

"Altered states?" Alex asked.

Dr. Kristatos turned to Alex. "My field is cryogenics, but I have fifteen years in the study of matter transformation—werewolf stuff, teeth into fangs, and so on. So I'm covering the department." She turned to Sangster. "But we do have an opening if you know an altered-state scientist who'd like to work underground on Lake Geneva."

Sangster put his hands in his pockets and shrugged. "Most of my friends are teaching *Huckleberry Finn*."

"And most of my friends are cutting his class," Alex said, shaking the woman's hand. Kristatos was two inches taller than Sangster and projected an air not unlike an Olympic giant herself. As she lowered her arm he saw her sleeve flutter and he caught a glimpse of the veins and sculpted muscles of her forearm.

"Where is he now?" Sangster asked.

Kristatos was shaking Astrid's hand, and Astrid seemed to bounce with extra enthusiasm as if to make up for the doctor's dryness; she kissed the woman on both cheeks, and Kristatos had to almost peel Astrid's hand off hers. "We're just transferring him to the interview tank." She gestured and urged them all to follow.

"If we hurry you might get to see the heat vent."

At once they were rushing to follow Kristatos's long strides as she unlocked and moved through three different metal-mesh-windowed doors. They passed labs and double doors to what Alex briefly made out to be holding cells.

Now the doctor stopped at a final blue door and looked at them, a darkened window revealing distant track lighting over her shoulder. "Check it out; I really think this is pretty amazing." She was human after all.

She pushed through the door and they all walked into a room the size of a two-car garage, with blue-gray concrete walls except for the back wall, which was glass. Alex stepped closer and saw that a glass wall separated them from the other half of the room.

Beyond the glass partition, the ceiling and floor were concrete but for a series of heavy-looking vents. It was a cage.

Alex saw what looked like scuba gear attached with suction cups to the inside of the cage. A mask with straps hung there, like he'd seen fighter pilots wear in the movies.

Within this room-within-the-shaft, visible through the glass partition, sat a tall chunk of ice that Alex had last seen on the night Icemaker almost killed him.

"Is that shatter-resistant glass?" Sangster asked.

Kristatos shook her head. "Plexiglas, and reinforced with silver."

"What's that?" Alex indicated a round black suction cup on the inside of the cage wall.

"It's a microphone."

"Don't forget," Sangster told Alex, "the quarry has been unconscious for three months, so remember this when you talk to him. Don't reveal any events he wouldn't already know about."

Alex nodded. He got it: As far as Icemaker was concerned, the Queen was still dead.

Kristatos spoke a code, fished a headset out of her pocket, recited another series of numbers and letters, and put the device away.

Alex went over to the wall and tapped on it, confused. "We're going to talk to the chunk of ice?"

Suddenly there was a sharp, loud *crack*, and Alex looked at the glass case in alarm.

"That's the heat from the air in the shaft," said Dr. Kristatos. "You might want to stand back."

"What? Why?" Alex stepped back, trying to follow the sounds. He saw water beginning to trickle out of a vent in the ceiling.

"Because I hate to admit it, but this is the first time we've ever tried this."

Water sprayed from the ceiling as though a pipe had

burst, and Alex heard an audible crack, distant and then sharpening as steam began to rise. A machine gun–like series of cracking sounds rattled beyond the glass as that section filled with steam.

Vents slammed open in the floor along the walls near Alex's feet, and Kristatos said, "Don't be alarmed. We're just venting the steam to relieve pressure so the cage doesn't explode."

For a moment, they were all enveloped in steam. Alex made out Astrid pulling out her staff and he tensed himself, feeling as though they were back in the soot and smoke of Vienna's pensione. A minute later, the steam began to thin, the haze opening, and the glass cage came once more into view.

Now it was full of milky fluid, mostly water, and there seemed to be water streaming down the front of it as well, maybe in some thin track between two panes. This gave the cage an even more dreamy appearance, and as Alex looked down at the vapor that still surrounded his feet, he felt completely isolated from the world as he knew it, even the crazy world he had come to know.

Alex heard Sangster blow out a long, steady breath he had clearly been holding in. Dr. Kristatos stood with them, and now even she seemed hesitant.

The milky, hazy cage, full from top to bottom with

water now, seemed empty, but the shadow moving in the back and the static howling in Alex's brain told him otherwise.

Astrid and Alex each stepped forward, reaching out an arm to block the other. The milky substance began to churn.

The creature that was Lord Byron slipped like a shark through the water and crashed into the glass wall. His black hair swirled in the water as he flattened his claw-like hands against the glass. His eyes were open, and he was looking straight at Alex.

Kristatos held out a small microphone to Sangster and the agent shook his head, gesturing toward Alex.

Alex tentatively took the device in his hand, running his finger over a *talk* button. He looked up at the vampire, who whipped his head slightly to whisk away a strand of hair. He seethed, his unbreathing mouth open in the milky water. He had his nails against the glass as though he were planning to claw through it.

"Well," Sangster said to Alex. "You wanted to talk to him. So talk."

CHAPTER 15

"Tell me again why the guy who uses water as his main source of power is in a water tank?" Alex whispered to Sangster and Kristatos.

"He uses *ice* as his power," Kristatos corrected him.

"Yeah, so shouldn't he be in, like, a dry sauna?"

"You don't need to whisper." The scientist looked at the vampire floating against the glass, watching them. "He can't hear us. But to answer your question, it's actually safer this way. By encasing him in a full tank, any freezing he does is likely to surround him with ice and overwhelm him."

"Likely?"

Kristatos breathed deeply and crossed her arms. "Well—"

"Look, we tried the sauna in the fifties, okay?" Sangster cut in.

"Okay, okay." Alex looked at his hands and thumbed the microphone. It was now or never. If he waited any longer, he was going to lose his nerve. The last time he had been this close to the vampire, Icemaker had been holding him aloft and starting to cut Alex's throat.

Click. "Hi, Byron."

In the water tank, the vampire looked startled for a brief moment, then recovered. He flapped his arms, floating back and searching the wall with what appeared to be an amused curiosity. Then Byron spotted the black apparatus and pilot's mask and floated toward it. He smiled a cruel, thin smile and made no attempt to respond.

Alex continued. "Long t—"

"Careful," Sangster whispered, and Alex keyed the mike off.

"What?"

"Byron has no idea how long he's been frozen; it's better not to reference time."

"Do *you* want to do this?"

"No. I'm actually sort of enjoying it like it is," Sangster replied.

Click. "I'd like to say I'm sorry to wake you."

"He can talk," Kristatos said. "If he puts on the mask."

Alex nodded, wondering how strange his voice must

sound coming from a speaker under the water. He looked at Byron. "If you want to answer—"

"Van Helsing." The voice came reedy and wet, burbling out of Byron's mouth as he held the mask to his face. He had figured it out instantly, and sounded bored already. Alex shuddered, feeling as though his name had just been spoken by an evil wave.

Don't you want to ask where you are? Alex thought, but he was looking in Byron's red eyes and realized that even if Byron did, he wouldn't ask outright. That would show vulnerability. Byron was determined to show that they had him exactly where he wanted them.

Byron drew back at once and tucked his head, preparing to ram the wall. Sangster quickly snatched the mike.

"There is a flowing stream of holy water on the other side of that glass. I wouldn't do that if I were you."

Byron stopped himself, floating there, and came back to the mike. "Clever," he uttered. He slipped the straps of the mask over his head so that it rested on his nose and mouth, leaving his hands free.

Sangster gave the mike back to Alex. *Why is he letting me do this?* Alex thought, not for the first time. He was always amazed that Sangster seemed eager to step out of the way.

Alex clicked on the mike again. "We want to ask you some questions."

There was another click. "Why should I answer your questions?" came the ghostly water-voice.

"Better accommodations," Sangster muttered.

"If you answer our questions, we might be able to move you into a better place." Alex spoke the words calmly, but he wasn't sure if they came across that way. He wasn't sure if it was true, and a bald lie could be difficult to mask.

Byron pursed his lips, swaying his head back and forth as if to say, *All right.* "What is it you want to know, little Van Helsing?"

"What do you know about the Dimmer Switch?"

Byron narrowed his eyes, studying Alex. "I'm not aware of anything called Dimmer Switch."

"You might know it as *Obscura Notte*," Alex said helpfully.

"Oh." Byron clapped his hands slowly, his arms sliding in the water. The gesture made his body bob in the milky substance. "Of course."

"Yes?"

"I first learned about Obscura Notte in 1935," he said.

Alex's ears pricked up and he leaned forward.

"Obscura Notte was the finest nightclub in all of

Italy." Byron laughed, creating a weird, gurgling sound in the mike.

"Hit it," Sangster said, and Kristatos stepped on a button near the wall. There was a coarse, sizzling sound as electricity shot through the water. Alex saw a million tiny particles of silver light up in the fluid, and Byron's body jolted uncontrollably. He raged at the glass as the shock died down.

Byron recovered as soon as the jolt passed, but it had made the point.

"I'm interested in real answers," Alex said dully. "Do you know anything about it or not?"

"The Triumph of Death." Byron was already composed, and when he clicked in, his gurgling voice sounded serene. "Why do you want to know?"

Alex looked at Sangster, who whispered, "Tell him it's a random vampire."

"There's a threat," Alex reported. "Some vampire is going to set it off. We want to know how to stop it."

"Old or new?" came the answer.

"What?"

"Is this an *old* vampire or a *new* vampire?"

Alex thought. "We don't know."

"Don't know or won't say?"

"We don't know."

"Well, then you're in trouble, because you need to know more." Byron sounded amused, mocking.

"Why?"

"Well, after all, the spell is called the Triumph of Death. The end of light, of living, of love. Only love can conquer death."

Alex frowned. "Come on. *You* conquered death. You're alive."

"We *are* death. There's a *difference*." Then Byron brought up his hand and a chunk of ice appeared in it, ready to shoot forward. But before it did, the ice went wild, shooting out in spirals around him. It encased his hand and he had to stop and pry the block off himself.

Now Alex understood how surrounding the Icemaker in water would foil him. There was too much water to control. Alex threw Kristatos an appreciative glance and she smiled slightly.

"Are you done?" Alex said into the mike. "So, go back—what do you mean, 'Only love can conquer death'?"

"Don't listen to me. I'm a poet."

"I thought vampires don't feel love."

"It's complicated."

"So if we know the person casting this spell, we can maybe . . . stop them from casting it?"

"Well, how well do you know them?" Byron asked.

Alex stared calmly.

"Good lord, you're thick," Byron said. "Your father and I spent three days chasing one another through the sewers of Paris. Talking to you, I get the impression you'd have been looking for me in the wrong city to begin with. What I'm saying is, if *you* were the one casting the spell, I would be able to stop you. Do you know why?"

"Change the subject," Sangster interrupted.

"You stop it by using the one whom the caster *loves*. So what I'm saying is that if it were *you*, I could absolutely stop it."

"Why's that, Byron?"

Byron put his hand flat on the glass, bringing his face forward. "Because I know you have a father who loves you. And a mother who loves you. And at least *three* of your four sisters love you. Don't they, Alex? What do you think I could do to use them against *you*?"

Alex found himself stepping forward, pointing at Byron. "What I think is that you're going to stay in this bath and shrivel up like a *raisin* while the world turns without you, you miserable excuse for a poet." He jabbed his finger against the glass.

As his fingertip touched the glass Byron's eyes flashed, and Alex almost heard the word *contact*.

He felt a burst of static and something was suddenly wrong with his finger; it was hard and brittle, and he started to scream and found that the static was screaming inside him already. Byron had his palm against the glass, and Alex could see a stream, a crack, a frozen trickle that went straight through the glass and hissed in the holy water in between. Something pulled at his head, as if the blood in his head and the water in the blood were a magnet and he was diving against his will. Alex's forehead smashed against the Plexiglas and he saw stars, blinding cold shooting through his brain. Byron had him.

In the distance, Sangster was yelling, pounding the electricity, and through a blue haze Alex saw Byron, laughing silently in the water, a whipping tentacle of ice a foot wide forming from Byron's hand, through cracked glass and hissing holy water, to Alex's forehead.

Ask the questions, Alex thought thickly, his vision a wild blur of spotted white.

I'm freezing . . . glass breaking . . .

What do you have?

Nothing.

Alex's vision swooped wild and he was looking at the ceiling, aware that glass chunks and ice were flying. He heard popping sounds, gunfire; Sangster must be shooting. Water was rushing over him and stalks of ice were flying through the room. He heard a woman scream and saw a pair of legs fall across his body. There seemed to be tentacles of ice flying in all directions as the water came over him. He tried to move but his neck was stiff, and the water came up over his nose.

Alex tried to blow air out of his nose, but the water came anyway and his sinuses screamed with pain. His vision snapped to for a moment, and he saw a blast of ice tear the door off its hinges, and he heard growling. He smelled burning flesh where bits of silver in the water sparked against Byron's chest.

Alex caught a glimpse of Astrid, swinging her green staff against Byron's neck, and Byron turned, punching her with a column of ice that sent her into a cement wall.

Suddenly Alex was being yanked up, and he thought *Sangster* and then was aware that a powerful claw had him by the chest, gripping his shirt, which was caked in ice.

Alex saw the vampire's fangs and felt blood gush from his neck.

Then, all went black.

CHAPTER 16

For a moment all Alex heard were voices and the slush of water rushing around his ears as he lay on the floor.

Forget Icemaker—

Kristatos?

Dead—

"*Alex?*" He heard Sangster call his name.

He blinked, light blazing into his eyes, and the shapes of Sangster and Astrid were washed out and filtered by light. There were red lamps flashing, and he had the delirious feeling he was in a nightclub.

What's happening?

"*You're on the ground. Get up.*"

His hands slipped under him and he tried to grip the

tiles with his fingers, and his fingers were sausages, bags of peanut butter. He saw the flickering of light as his eyes blinked rapidly, and he was unable to stop them.

" . . . *pressure on it!*" Sangster shouted, and then he saw Astrid move over him, clamping her hand down on his throat. Something that looked black gushed toward her.

He was being carried, then he felt himself slamming down onto something like a bed.

"Out of the way. Where is the infirmary?" he heard Sangster call. A shadow of a scientist shouted something. There was blood on the walls, and Alex held his eyes open long enough to see a gash in the ceiling tiles, dripping with water, where something had punched clear through and kept going.

They turned a corner and the lights kept flickering.

"I'm sorry!" he rasped. "I'm sorry I went out!"

"Don't worry about that now," came Astrid's voice. She brought her other hand to his forehead and leaned in close. "I'm here because of you. Don't leave."

Something squishy and oily crossing his forehead and dissolving under Astrid's thumb. A flare, a burst of phosphorous. Unknown, ancient words. Then, darkness washed over him.

In the distance he heard voices:

Astrid's voice. *I have to take him.*

Sangster: *Absolutely not—*

He has been bitten very badly. I can help him. We can help him.

He belongs with us.

You don't know the first thing about who he belongs with! You have to trust me. There is no time. The poison will start to work the curse, and you know as well as I do that he will not survive it, and we will not allow this Van Helsing—this Van Helsing—to die without doing everything in our power.

Where?

The Orchard.

A voice next to his ear. *Alex. Hold my hand. Mother Gretel, we are coming to you.*

Darkness stayed. Within it he listened to the hissing of the oil on his forehead. He began hallucinating.

He was falling now, the ground opening up, and he was falling down a tree, sunlight streaming through shadow leaves.

Alex!

Something caustic struck the air under his nose and ignited his sinuses, and his eyes shot open.

Suddenly awake, Alex screamed in pain, trying to reach for his neck as he looked up to see Astrid. He couldn't move his arms.

He was outside, in an orchard of red and yellow fruit trees, below a canopy of brightly colored leaves and a cloudless sky. He was lying in a clearing on a tilted wooden table of some kind, and when he tried to move his arms again he saw that they were bound by a rope-like, shimmering green light.

Astrid touched his arm. "It's for your own good."

"Tell him not to struggle," came an older female voice, and Alex's eyes darted to the edge of the clearing, where a woman with white hair was searching through a brown wooden bureau that had leaves growing out of it. "Tell him it'll only make the poison move faster."

Alex studied the bureau and the leaves some more and looked at Astrid. "Where am I?"

"Alex, listen to me," Astrid said. "You've been bitten very badly. Are you listening?"

Alex blinked. "Yes."

"You were bitten fifteen minutes ago. We got here as fast as we could."

"Where's here?" Alex tried to wrestle against the magical cords and suddenly felt achingly weak.

"You're in the Orchard."

"The Orchard?"

Leaves whipped up and the woman who had been at

the bureau now stood at his side, across from Astrid. "You're in the home of Hexen." The woman appeared old, at first, deep creases around her eyes and mouth, and then when her face moved, the lines seemed to smooth away. She seemed to move in a slow blur.

Ignore that. What's going on?

"Icemaker bit me on the neck." Alex's mind raced. "Am I bleeding out?"

Astrid shook her head. "No, no, no, you really haven't lost too much—he missed the artery, but the poison will start working on you, and you're as good as dead if we don't do what we have to do."

"That doesn't sound good at all." Alex looked down, amazed at the blood that had spilled across his shirt.

The old woman passed a hand over his shirt and the color changed, the blood smoothing away with her touch. "These details will not burden you."

She moved to the side and turned to another table that he hadn't noticed before, with a silver tray lying in the center of it. Next to this was a set of small clay pots. Black powder lay in the center of the silver tray, and when she waved a hand, the powder ignited. A black tendril of smoke began to rise and fill the clearing.

"Venus or Mars?" The woman turned to Astrid. "Love or war, which will heal him best now?"

"I don't know. Why would you ask me?"

"You're supposed to know him by now."

"To have protected him, is that what you mean?" Astrid shot back, her face red. "I know."

Alex felt something sharp race up and down the back of his neck, as though he'd been spattered with fire, and he gasped.

Astrid was at his ear again, whispering. *Mother Gretel, you protect us,* Astrid said. *You take away the pain.* She looked back at the old woman. "The poison is moving fast, Mother Laura." Her eyes raced. "War, it has to be."

The woman called Mother Laura clucked her tongue and started moving items from the buckets. "We need euphorbium, bdellium, root of hellebore . . . got a lodestone here, good." She looked at Astrid. "Go get me a vial of blood of cat, would you?"

Astrid disappeared to the bureau and shot back with a vial of dark liquid that Mother Laura threw into the silver tray. The smoke had changed now, billowing red.

Astrid turned back to Alex. "This is called 'suffumigation of Mars'; it will envelop you in healing mist."

"But it lacks the blood that we need—the blood that matters," said Mother Laura.

The stinging feeling in Alex's neck was making his

body shake. He was beginning to hurt more. He was having trouble following what the witches were saying.

Alex looked at Astrid and suddenly she seemed to burble, her skin becoming translucent, and Alex saw blood flowing through her veins beneath her skin.

"I'm seeing blood." Alex blinked. "I see your blood."

"That's the poison working in you." Astrid's eyes darted as she studied Alex. "It's making you see as a vampire sees."

"Get it out!" he tried to roar, but his voice was hoarse and sounded distant to himself.

"We need the blood of one who loves him," Mother Laura said. "Even for war, we need love."

Astrid looked at her. She shook her head. "What, me?"

Mother Laura actually smirked. "Oh, please, child, I don't mean you." She turned to Alex, who by now was having a hard time focusing on her, the pain in his muscles screaming, and the woman was flickering into a creature whose blood he could practically taste. "Alex," Mother Laura said, "you are in the Orchard of Hexen. All who pass through here carry a little of it with them. And they will hear you and come if you call to them."

Alex couldn't make her words string together into any kind of thought at all. He arched his back and screamed.

Somewhere, someone heard him.

Alex's eyes were flickering with pain and darkness as he saw a curtain in the air open up between two fruit trees.

He caught the silhouette of a woman in a leather coat and a floppy brown hat, pulling off a pair of long gloves with a familiar deftness.

"What is it you want me to do?" came the voice of Amanda Van Helsing, his mother, as he lost consciousness.

CHAPTER 17

Alex awoke with a start, looking into a cloudless sky, with a light breeze fluttering across a thin, green wool blanket draped over his body. He found he was able to move, and he sat up and felt the cot he was lying on sag under his body. He was still in the Orchard he had been in earlier, but the wooden table and the bureau were nowhere to be seen.

Without a watch, without a clock, without a phone, he felt thoroughly disoriented. How long had he been asleep? Hours? *Days?*

Alex pulled the blanket off his legs. He was wearing a pair of plain black trousers and a cream-colored shirt, and a pair of light slip-on shoes lay at the edge of the cot.

There was a full-length mirror on wooden feet next to the cot, with a small table and washbasin. As he looked in the mirror, Alex saw his neck was covered in a bandage, but as he touched it he found that the wound underneath felt superficial. For a moment he picked at the adhesive edges and began to peel it back, then thought better of it.

He scanned the clearing. "Hello?"

Alex stood up, studying the trees. He was looking deep into the Orchard, trying to find any other people, but he could see no one. He began to walk, moving past the bed and mirror and stepping between two trees.

Suddenly he was standing in a train station and nearly run over by a baggage cart. He spun around and looked at the glass-and-metal station door he'd stepped through and saw the Orchard beyond, and ripped the door back open before he even knew what he was doing.

He was back in the Orchard.

Alex put out his arms, then, feeling for some kind of balance or edge of reality. He felt dizzy and wondered if he'd been given hallucinatory pain medication.

He was injured; he remembered that. And he had been taken . . . here? He went back to the cot and then looked down at the unfamiliar black pants he was wearing.

"We burned your clothes," Astrid said, and Alex suddenly turned to see her emerging from between two trees about twenty feet away. "One of the weavers had a set that she'd made for a son of one of the cooks. I hope they fit."

"Where did you come from?" He stared at Astrid and shook his head. "I don't understand this orchard," he said. Then he gestured at the multicolored fruits on one of the trees. "And what's this fruit?"

"Knowledge." Astrid laughed. "It's how we store knowledge."

"Um," he ran his fingers through his hair. "I'm sorry. How long was I asleep?"

"About a day," she said. "It's Thursday."

He felt the electric jolt of the lateness of the hour. "Thursday, God, we're losing time. Where is everyone— I thought I saw . . ." He wasn't sure how pathetic this would sound. "I could swear I saw my mother."

Astrid nodded brightly. "Yes! She's still here. Come on, we're having a meeting, and we were hoping you'd be awake and able to join." She gestured for him to follow, and as they stepped between the two trees from which she'd come, the scene changed.

They were walking down a corridor of marble tile with heavy wood-paneled walls. Alex looked back and saw that he'd just come through a simple wooden doorway, and beyond it he could still see the trees and the cot. "Was the room an illusion, like a hologram?"

"What?" Astrid stopped next to a painting on the wall, a portrait of a woman with a feathered hat and a blue blouse. Underneath it a plaque read M. BRELAZ, PORTUGAL.

"I mean it was a clearing in an orchard. No walls and no ceiling, and now we're in a building," Alex said, working out how he'd try to build such a thing. "So was it, like, a room with holographic walls, maybe a movie screen on the ceiling?"

"Maybe the hallway is the illusion," Astrid said mysteriously as they walked farther, passing numerous doors, each wooden, each with a silver plate at the center that marked them with what Alex assumed to be numbers, probably in the Hexen language. Astrid stopped finally at a door and turned back. "I'm just teasing you," she said, opening the door. "It's all practical and physical, but there's magic in the way it's all connected."

They stepped into an enormous den that reminded Alex of a ski lodge, with huge windows looking out on snowy mountains, large wooden chandeliers, and a massive fireplace. A round table sat on the stone tiles of the room, and Alex saw the white-haired woman he had met earlier sitting at one of a number of high-backed chairs. In front of her was a plate of fruit, and next to her was a large wheel with an enormous spool of thread perched on top—a spinning wheel.

Alex's mother, Amanda, was standing at the table sliding her hand over a leather parchment, flicking her fingers the way you might flick the screen on an iPhone. "Look at that, he sleeps late even in the most hidden space in the world."

"Mom." Alex smiled at the sight of his mother, and ran and embraced her, and then pulled back and said, "Wait—the way it's connected?"

Amanda turned to Astrid. "You were explaining the layout of Hexen?"

"I was trying," Astrid said.

Amanda chewed her lip and turned back to Alex. "You want the spiritual answer or the practical one?"

"Would I understand the spiritual answer?"

"Well, it's more true, but here's the practical one," Alex's mom said. "The headquarters of Hexen are distributed throughout the world and stitched together through concentrated magical couplings."

"Is there . . . a map?"

Mother Laura, the woman who had been there when Alex was writhing with pain, was jotting something in a notebook and lifted her pencil. "Since you ask, there is a map, but it's complicated, and we're a little behind in updating it."

"Wasn't the committee . . . ," Amanda started to ask.

"Oh, they forgot the Pentagon." Laura waved a hand dismissively.

"That's a broom closet in the 1940s," Amanda scoffed.

"It anchors the whole northern edge," Laura protested. "The map makes no sense without it. It has to be recast entirely."

"I'll pass on the map," Alex said. "I'm sorry—I'm having a hard time understanding any of this. I didn't even know there was a Hexen until Astrid showed up to help us with Claire. I didn't know my mother was a part of it." He looked at his mother. "Or—*is* a part of it. Are you still in this?"

"Sometimes." Amanda bobbed her head. "I wasn't born into it, though; I was recruited as a child in New York. But allow me to introduce Mother Laura, who currently leads the organization."

Laura nodded to Alex. The white-haired woman was wearing a lavender blouse and a cameo like the one that Astrid carried. "Your mother is leaving out that when she came to us she was already one of the most gifted adepts we'd ever seen. I trust you're doing better?"

Alex nodded. "Are there any others?"

"There are hundreds," Laura responded. "All over the world, and just through that door."

"We were founded by Mad Meg," Astrid said.

"Mad Meg?"

"You know the story of Gretel, like in Hansel and Gretel? Gretel was the one who didn't give up when she faced the witch. She was the one who figured out how to defeat the witch and finally did the work of kicking her into the furnace. Gretel, the one who decided to use everything she'd learned and form a house of witches who would fight for good. That childhood story, that wasn't the end of it, you know. When she was an adult she was the one to raise an army of women in Germany to open the gates of hell and win back her loved ones. She had a different name at that time—Mad Gretel. Mad Meg, some called her."

Alex thought of Astrid's name. "You're Astrid Gretelian. So you're *related* to Gretel?"

"Yes, my family are direct descendants of Mad Meg, the first Gretel." She smiled, sipping her tea. "Somewhere back there, anyway."

"Astrid's one of those born into Hexen," Amanda said. "Powerful adeptness just flows right down her bloodline."

"Wait," Alex said. "When you were here last month, you said you knew I was in trouble because you were meditating with another witch and she called your attention to the danger."

"That's right," his mom answered.

"So you literally could be having a . . . session with a protégé from anywhere in the world."

"Right!" Amanda said. "That's why it's not so bad living in the middle of nowhere."

Alex became aware of Astrid smiling next to him and he pointed to her. "And you're the protégé." Astrid simply waved.

Alex shook his head. "Oh, come on, Mom! Seriously? You set me up? With a witch?"

"No, Alex," Amanda said. "It's not a setup. There was no better person to send to work with you. And only you merited a partner from the Orchard."

Alex still wasn't used to the idea that his mom was not just a witch but part of a community, an active part the way his father had been active with the Polidorium. As Alex considered this, he felt once more the mix of anger and betrayal and pride that he'd felt when he first saw pictures of his father fighting vampires before Alex was born. Anger and betrayal because both Amanda and Charles had insisted while Alex was growing up that there were *no such things* as vampires, werewolves, witches, or anything of that nature. But, in fact, *Talia sunt, there are such things.* They had decided to protect him by keeping the truth from him, even as Amanda allowed Charles to train Alex in every skill he would need when the time came to join the war.

That whole jumble of emotion, the anger and betrayal and pride, mixed in a kind of jagged, giddy excitement now. He was too happy to see her to be angry, too proud to be part of them to feel betrayed.

"Only me . . . because of my power, the static thing I have?"

"Give me some credit, Alex," Amanda said. "I was also calling in a favor for my son, because the Polidorium was about to go up against Claire Clairmont."

"You were . . . worried about me?"

Amanda scoffed. "Oh, come on. Of course I was worried. Just last month I almost forced you to come home. Yes. I was worried."

"What about Dad . . . does he know about this whole thing?"

"He knows I'm here, and he knows I'm helping you."

"He really is serious about staying out," Alex said. "So you coming here didn't merit him strapping on the old Polibow?"

"He never had a Polibow, but he's not strapping anything on as long as we have children at home. That's the deal."

Alex was struck by the fact that his father might not have wanted to retire; this had never occurred to him. "What about you?"

"It's not the same."

"Well." Alex looked around at the room. "I mean, the décor is different, but don't you think it kind of seems the same?"

"It's not," Amanda said. "I promise."

"Shall we get started?" Mother Laura cleared her throat and bade Alex and Astrid sit.

"Lights," said Laura, and the windows darkened and lights dimmed as she picked up one of the pieces of parti-colored fruit. She turned to her spinning wheel and stabbed the fruit onto a spike above the wheel, and he heard wooden pedals begin to move at her feet.

For a moment the fruit dripped as the wheel spun, and then a line of thread shot through the air and began to mound upon itself at the center of the table.

"What's this?" Alex whispered to Astrid.

"I said earlier that we store our knowledge in the fruit," Astrid said. "We read the fruit by extracting the juice onto thread from the wheel."

"Why can't you just read the fruit?"

"Can *you* read fruit?" she asked with an arched eyebrow. "It's easier with the thread."

"So . . . what do you do with the thread?" Alex was wondering if Mother Laura was going to knit them a readable sweater.

"Alex, just watch," Amanda whispered. Then she patted Astrid's knee as if she felt sorry for her.

The thread stacked, and flowed, and soon formed into an image about three feet high. Washed-out color came into the image, spotted with fluid and bits of wool. It was a three-dimensional model of a woman with curly brown hair, about forty years old. The woman looked like a Russian countess, with a long white coat and white muff.

"Claire Clairmont during her Russia years." Mother Laura kept pedaling, the thread looping around her, lying in wait. "This is the woman who is currently threatening the world."

Amanda went on. "Claire came to Hexen in 1827 while she worked in Russia as a governess. She possessed great powers of suggestion and seduction and was trained by the organization to be placed in the Russian court as a spy. But of course she had no intention of continuing with us. What she really wanted was to find

Lord Byron, her lover, who by that time was an active vampire with the Scholomance, and reunite her family. Most of all, she wanted Allegra."

Another image appeared next to Claire's, coming to about her waist, a little girl with lush blond curls: Allegra Byron.

Laura picked up the story. "Allegra Byron was born in 1817 and was immediately taken in by Lord Byron, her father, who proceeded to deny Claire any access. He was willing to have Allegra in his life, but he was irritated by Claire and found sadistic pleasure in keeping them apart. But Byron soon tired of Allegra and had the little girl placed in a convent in Italy, where she died at the age of five, of typhus."

Another image grew, a tall and sneering image Alex knew well. "And this is Lord Byron, the vampire you call Icemaker. We think that sometime in the 1830s, Byron and Claire reconciled. These two people, Byron and the little Allegra, are the most important people in Claire's life."

Another image grew, a man with a beard in a simple shirt and floppy hat. "This is Pieter Bruegel, the painter."

Astrid cut in. "I learned in Madrid that Pieter Bruegel was paid to create a painting to commemorate the actual effects of the spell known as the Triumph of Death. The people who hired him were located in a castle of huge black towers. The painting contains clues as to how to stop the curse."

"Yes," Mother Laura said. "Blacktowers, that's a group as old as Hexen."

Alex's head was spinning with the idea that the Polidorium, whose roots he always regarded as ancient, was actually quite young compared to some of these older players in the game. "We've been calling them the Strangers," Alex said. "And they're still active. Updating the painting as they go. Even leading us to the clues in case we missed them."

A bird-like chirp drew Alex's glance to a paneled wall opposite the large windows. The wooden slats there spun around slowly and clicked back into place, forming a wall-sized flat panel of gray. The gray panel flickered, and Alex looked through the wall and saw the Polidorium boardroom.

Sangster and Armstrong were in the boardroom looking at them, and on the screen at the end of their table, Alex could see they were again looking at the painting, *The Triumph of Death.*

"Mother Laura?" Sangster said, standing up. "Thank you for answering. I don't think we've formally met."

"Well, there's no time like the present," Mother Laura replied.

Alex looked at Astrid. "Wait, how did they—" Alex

shook his head. "Is this magic, too?"

"It's Cisco Telepresence." Laura smiled and looked back at Sangster. That was sophisticated teleconferencing software. So that meant that when they preferred it, Hexen had any kind of tech it wanted in the Orchard. Nice. "You've found something?"

"Maybe," Sangster said. "Alex, how are you feeling?"

"I . . . I guess I'm glad to be here," he said.

Now Sangster smiled, genuinely. "Not many people can survive an attack from a vampire as powerful as Byron. It was a close call."

Alex swallowed and tried to decide what to say. "It shouldn't have happened. I let him get to me."

"That's all the more reason to count your blessings."

Alex nodded several times, but he was uncomfortable with the attention. Icemaker would kill thousands in the years to come, he was sure of it. Even if they stopped the Triumph of Death. Alex had committed an atrocity by being the vehicle for Byron's escape. He was caught for a minute in a loop of self-disgust.

"Alex?" Sangster said.

"Sir?"

"Set it aside."

Alex ran his hand through his hair and nodded again.

"While you were out, we got more from Madrid."

Sangster indicated the image of the painting on the screen. "Remember how the painting was tampered with? There were at least two other places in the painting where colors had been changed. One in the bottom corner—the blue skirts of the lover. And two more—a red cloak made blue around the center, and another cloak made blue in the upper right."

"So a lot of cloaks altered to be blue," Alex said.

"Exactly." Sangster looked at Alex, watching him. He hit a button on the table and said, "I'm sharing an image with you guys." At once a quarter of the screen filled with another painting, this one a strange, colorful image of countless figures in a medieval courtyard. Alex read the caption underneath. "*Netherlandish Proverbs*."

"Same painter as *The Triumph of Death*: Pieter Bruegel, 1562. But this painting has another name besides *Netherlandish Proverbs*."

Alex read the smaller text underneath the name. "*The Blue Cloak.*" Alex searched the painting. There had to be thirty or forty characters, walking, trading, talking, taking care of animals. It was a busy street scene. "Why is it called *The Blue Cloak*?"

Amanda, who had taught art history as recently as last year, spoke up from her side of the room. "The painting is a visual collection of famous sayings. For instance there's a guy petting a chicken, and that stands for 'being a hen feeler,' which was another phrase for 'Don't count your chickens before they hatch.'"

"There's your cloak," Alex said, finding the image of a woman standing behind a man, putting a blue cloak over his head.

"To put the cloak over someone was to deceive them, to pull the wool over their eyes," said Amanda.

"Okay." Alex had given up trying to argue that their faith in the riddle-makers might be misplaced. It was all they had for now. "So the alterations the Strangers made to *The Triumph of Death* lead us to *The Blue Cloak*. Is this clue telling us something about deception?"

"Well, *The Blue Cloak* is about deception." Sangster swiped his hand and brought up *The Blue Cloak*, aka *Netherlandish Proverbs* on the main screen. "But that's not the mystery."

"And there *is* a mystery?"

"There is indeed. Art historians have identified no fewer than forty different sayings in the painting. Every detail—every animal and every prop *means* something in this painting. Except that there is one strange item that doesn't seem to fit. This *hoe*." Sangster zoomed the image to the center right area, until an image of a garden hoe without a handle lying on a table came into view.

Alex mused. "What good is a hoe without a handle? Isn't that what it means?"

"Sure, if you want to guess, but the rest of these are all extremely deliberate. There isn't any Netherlandish proverb about a hoe without a handle."

"And there's more," Armstrong offered.

"What is it?" Alex asked. "I mean, forty actual sayings and you're focusing on the non-saying?"

Mother Laura nodded. "What did Byron tell you about the curse?"

Alex searched through what they had learned from Byron before he got Alex's goat and managed to escape. He closed his eyes, shifting everything back, bringing the problem to the front. "'Only love can conquer death.' He said if I were casting the spell he could stop me because he knew who I loved."

Laura said, "The one the user loves best is the best weapon against him."

"Well," Alex said, "Claire loved Byron. And she's going to get him back, because we just set him free."

"And of course"—Laura nodded toward the image of the child—"there is another, greater love."

"When Claire traveled to Russia and secretly joined Hexen," Astrid said, "she remained convinced that her daughter could be restored to her. She was obsessed with the idea that Byron had maybe even secreted away the little girl."

"We have letters," Sangster went on, "from the embalmer to Byron, demanding to be paid. He thought Byron was a complete jackass who wasn't even willing to come visit his daughter. The body was sent back without Byron even looking at it."

"So the Triumph is really Claire's way to raise her daughter from the dead," Alex said.

Sangster countered, "And it also means her daughter is the best weapon against her."

"So we can stop Claire by using someone who Claire loves—we can make a weapon, maybe. Maybe with DNA," Alex said excitedly. "From the bones of Allegra."

"You mean a weapon like this?" Armstrong set down something on the table that looked like a starter gun with a large section of its barrel hollowed out. She held up a glass vial next to the weapon. "You're right, Alex, the weapon will be DNA, shot straight into the heart of Claire. To do that, this is what we would use: It's a vial gun—you load it with vials that hold a compartment of holy water and a compartment of whatever you want to mix the water with." She tilted it sideways. "There's a hammer in here that breaks the vials, mixing them and then pressurizing the mixture for firing."

Alex nodded.

"We would like to see this body of Allegra as well," Mother Laura said, nodding to Astrid. "We might learn things from it."

"Okay, so you have your reasons, and we have something to shoot—we just need to find Allegra," Alex said. "And we have—*ugh*—three days. Where was the body sent?"

"To the churchyard of Byron's school in England, a place called Harrow," Sangster said.

Alex had heard of Harrow. That was a boys' school in England, one of the very best. He didn't know much else.

Sangster nodded. "And there's another word for *Harrow*."

"Let me guess," Alex said. "The one thing the painting points to: a hoe."

CHAPTER 18

Alex and Astrid's trip back to the Polidorium took
no time. One minute, they were saying good-bye to
Amanda and hurrying back to the Orchard, and the
next minute, they stepped through a pair of trees and
emerged near the public library in Secheron village.

"It's useful to have a drop-off point here," Astrid said.

"Conveniently near school but not so close as to be
suspicious. It's like a bus stop. When you brought me
to the Orchard before, did we come through here?" He
was so out of it when his blood was draining away after
Icemaker's attack that he had no memory of the trip.

"No," Astrid said. "I used a more powerful and tiring
spell, a direct jump to the Orchard. It takes a lot out of
you. This is easier."

Astrid summoned her motorcycle near their drop-off point and they rode from the village back to the farmhouse. Alex felt a throb of guilt as they headed into the woods, leaving the road that he would have used on a normal day to go back to school. He needed to call Paul, Sid, and Minhi. But there wasn't time. From conference table to conference table, from the world of magic to the world of spies, the trip took twenty-six minutes.

It was then another three hours flying from the airfield near the farmhouse before they reached the final resting place of Allegra Byron. With a cold gray wind sweeping off the Thames, Alex rested his hand on a low stone wall and took in the trees that curled over the graveyard like arthritic fingers.

In the months that Alex had been chasing vampires, he had rarely had occasion to visit that eternal vestige of vampire films and books—the churchyard. Now, as he, Sangster, Armstrong, and Astrid got out of the Polidorium van, he found himself in the kind of churchyard seen in movies—tombstones hundreds of years old and creeping with moss, scattered shade from London ash trees, and a massive, crawling, weeping elm that threatened to swallow the graveyard whole. Alex shivered and brought his jacket closer against the wind that snapped over the crumbling walls around St. Mary's Churchyard at Harrow in northwest London. Not counting wherever the Orchard was, this was the fourth country he had visited in under a week.

His mother had left the Orchard the same way Alex and Astrid had, and he assumed she had stepped out in either Wyoming or a broom closet in the Pentagon in the 1940s; at this point, he had no way of knowing. But it was no wonder to him that Hexen didn't let the Polidorium come visit. That place could have dangerous uses.

"Over here," Sangster called. Alex followed Sangster's voice and found the agent standing next to a low-slung tombstone erected against a wall. Astrid and Armstrong followed, and Alex dropped down to read the inscription on the stone:

In memory of Allegra, daughter of G. G., Lord Byron, who died at Bagna Cavallo in Italy, April 20, 1822, Aged Five Years and Three Months. "I shall go to her, but she shall not return to me."
—2 Samuel, xii, 23.

Alex sighed.

"That was put up in 1980 by the Byron Society," Sangster said.

"Nineteen eighty? So what was here before?" Alex asked.

Astrid cut in. "Nothing. There was no marker for Allegra's grave because Lord Byron refused to pay for one, and Claire had no money. Claire complained about this, though she never visited the grave."

Alex rubbed his forehead, looking uncomfortable. "I don't know."

"What?"

"What we're gonna do. I mean, you're talking about desecrating a grave here."

As if reminded by Sangster, Armstrong began unfolding a tripod of sorts that she drew from a bag. Within moments, she was clicking buttons and aiming a camera that hung from the bottom of the tripod at the grass.

Sangster sighed. "We worked all morning, we pulled every string, and we have the permits to exhume this body and take a sample for study purposes."

"But that's not what we're doing," Alex whispered, suddenly hoping no officials from the nearby church were listening. In the distance he heard singing, Anglican hymns at a late-morning service. "We're talking about using the body of a woman's dead child against her. This is just . . . it's too much."

"We followed the clues, Alex. This is where they lead. If you can think of a better way to stop the Triumph I'd love to hear it, but we are absolutely, genuinely running out of time."

Alex stamped his feet lightly, pulling his coat closer against the biting wind. Allegra Byron, five years old, had been kept from an obsessed mother and left by an uncaring father to die in a convent. And now they were going to use that tragedy, take a scrape of tissue, and build a weapon. He wished he could stop and bring Paul, Sid, and Minhi here. Something told him they wouldn't like this plan, either. It was darker than they would associate with him. It was darker than he liked to associate with himself.

But the alternative was worse: a *world* plunged into darkness. They would take a scrape of the dead in order to stave off death. It was necessary, but it didn't make him feel any better.

"How are we going to do it?" Alex asked.

Armstrong was peering into a small device with what looked like a GPS screen on it. "I see the coffin. We're looking at a depth of about seven feet, no surprise. The dense shadow inside, I'm assuming that's the body, which would have been wrapped head to toe in bandages."

"Okay, let us know when you're near." Sangster turned to answer Alex. "We'll do it the way we always do. We're bringing in a backhoe and we're tearing the place up."

"A backhoe?" Alex was incredulous. "Isn't that a little . . ."

"Low tech?" Sangster said.

"Yeah, I mean, everything else we do is on hyperdrive; even our motorcycle rearview mirrors are special."

"Hm." Sangster squinted. "You know, a few years ago I had my wisdom teeth extracted? So, the dentist has all kinds of crazy stuff. Lasers for oral surgery, and a million kinds of anesthetic. Music piping into your headset, and a chair that should have been designed by NASA. But you wanna know what it takes to actually take out the tooth?"

Alex shrugged.

"A hammer and a chisel," Sangster said. "Some things just don't change very fast. Anyway, it's not like we can beam the body out."

Alex nodded and began to wander away, looking up at the church, with its spire threatening to slice through the gray blanket of sky. He couldn't stay here for this. "Astrid, you want to have a look at the church with me?"

She bobbed her head yes, and they followed a mossy path up to the entrance of the church. A pair of red doors set inside a stone archway flapped open as parishioners began to stream out.

Alex thrust his hands into his coat pockets as he and Astrid stepped into the church itself, taking in the long central nave and transepts, with columns from front to back. The parishioners were chattering all around Alex and Astrid in accents that reminded Alex of Paul, who seemed even farther away than he was.

As they walked along the back of the last pew, Alex slid his hand along the soft, carved wood and whispered, "I wanted to ask you a question."

"Oh?" Astrid shrugged, following him. She had been curiously quiet lately, since his bite. The chatty front she put up had slid away, or at least seemed to be put away, waiting for a safer, happier time to come out.

"Whose idea was it to *not* tell me that you were a friend of my mother's?" Quickly, flatly; he wanted to get the words out.

"Alex . . ."

"When we met, you said you were here because of Claire. Because Hexen wanted to keep track of one of their fallen witches."

"That's true."

"But don't you think you could have told me from the start, 'Hey, Alex, get this, I know your mom, she's my mentor! She thought I'd be perfect for this gig!'"

"It wasn't like that. . . ."

"Wasn't it? You saved my life; that was the first thing you did. I thought maybe you were being nice. But you're on an assignment, and your assignment was to spy on me." He looked up at the ceiling, finding carvings so intricate he could barely comprehend them.

"Not to spy on you," she corrected. "To partner with you. And anyway, isn't it enough that I *did* save your life?"

"For my mom and her pals, no less, which is all kinds of troubling," Alex said. "I mean, when you think of it this way, why not tell the truth up front? Because you wanted to get close to me. Isn't that it? You wanted me to like you, to feel like I was, I was . . . special, that we were on this adventure. Together."

"You are special."

"Not. Like. *That*," Alex spat. Some parishioners looked at him. He lowered his voice. "Do you know what I was before I came to Switzerland, to Glenarvon? I was a stupid kid. I hiked and climbed mountains and my dad told me that the world was one way and all these other things were not a part of it. And then I come here, and suddenly, you know what I am? Special. *Very* special. I'm a tool, Astrid. A pawn. And you dragged me away from my friends, who *like* me for being . . . something else. Something not so special."

"I don't think you could avoid being special."

"Ugh, that's . . ." Alex blinked, trying not to look in her eyes. He stood up straight then, and after a moment spoke again. "Look, Astrid. I get that this is your job, even more than the Polidorium is mine. I think maybe that shows me a way that—don't take this the wrong way—that I don't want to go. Sangster calls the shots and I don't—so we're here, and we're gonna desecrate a grave, and then we're gonna stop the bad guys. And after that, I don't think your assignment of spying on me is gonna be very interesting, because I can't do this anymore. I'm out."

He turned around, about to walk dramatically away, but suddenly the church and the lamps and the light outside all went out at once.

CHAPTER 19

A curious humming sound came warbling from the churchyard as Alex and Astrid ran out into what had become a reddish night. Alex swept the surroundings of the hill with his eyes and found none of the sights that had been visible before—down the hill stood no Wembley Stadium or modern structures of any kind. Instead, a vista of distant, fiery darkness surrounded them like a curtain, projecting images of cities and ships ablaze.

"They're using it again," Alex shouted as he and Astrid rounded the bend. The vampires had set off the same spell they had used in Secheron, allowing them to create a limited, enclosed night. Seeing it working a second time, he had some idea how terrible a world enveloped in it would be. He nearly ran into a parishioner with gray hair and glasses, who was muttering a name, wandering in the darkness. Alex put his wireless into his ear as he ran and tapped it. "Sangster, where are you?"

There was no answer. Alex heard the burst of gunfire and saw the muzzles of Sangster's and Armstrong's Berettas lighting up down the hill, next to a wall. That was when he saw the skull faces of vampires in service of the Queen.

Sangster's voice sounded in Alex's ear. "Don't worry about us. Protect the grave."

Fifty yards away, Sangster was pinned against a low wall by a vampire in red robes. Armstrong was nearby, atop the wall Sangster was against, and she was kicking at a vampire that stood toe to toe with her. Sangster's foe leapt up on the short wall not far behind Armstrong, and the vampire had Sangster by the neck. For a moment Alex saw Sangster's legs leave the ground, struggling. Then there was a series of shots and the vampire exploded over the agent. Alex saw Sangster stand up and look back up the path at him. Armstrong flipped over the wall with her opponent and then there was another explosion of dust. "This way!" Sangster shouted to the other parishioners that were wandering still, screaming. He pointed at the false horizon, which hung in the air and blocked the view of the daytime world beyond. "This way to the road! Look! Those burning buildings, that's fake! It's just a movie projected on a—a curtain; you can walk right through it!"

Alex's attention was caught by Astrid, who had stopped at the next wall that led into the heart of the churchyard with Allegra's grave. She was standing still, shaking her head, a strange, thin silhouette against the distant curtain of red and black. "What is it?" he called, and then he was at her side and saw.

Several images hit Alex at once, and at first he had no idea which to focus on.

There were two vampires, their faces painted like skulls, holding a child of about six or seven, one of the parishioners, by the arms. Their white arms rippled with blue veins and their nails were digging in as they squeezed her tightly by the wrists.

That flooding in your chest. It tells everyone else to be afraid and lose their stuff. It reminds you, if you let it, to slow down. Slow down. Take it in.

The vampires were staring at him, and Astrid and Alex ignored them for a second, daring to look away from the girl. Just a few yards beyond the screaming little girl in the green coat and the matching green hat, something strange was happening at the grave.

There was dirt flying, churning as if being rotor-tilled. At first it looked as though there were a great wheel moving of its own accord, but then Alex heard it breathing, seething and hissing with exertion. It was a creature half submerged in the soft earth, its great legs churning around and around, and each time its legs emerged from the ground, he saw its powerful claws, and saw it toss back a mound of earth. The creature had a bulbous, bald head and white, boiled-egg eyes, its skin a reddish tone made even more devilish by the strange gleam of the curtain of night.

Alex searched his brain. He had seen it before. It was a vampire of some kind, one of the ones he had learned about. It was known to dig up crops and spread plague.

"What is that?" Astrid asked.

"I am blanking on the name," Alex said, wishing he had Sid with him. Sid would know as surely as Dr. DeKamp would. "But it's digging up Allegra's grave. Why would they be doing that?" Alex asked, but then it was obvious. If the Queen was vulnerable to DNA from her most beloved, she would want to get it before they did.

"We need to—" Astrid started to say.

"No closer," one of the vampires hissed. "I don't even have to say why."

Alex didn't look at the vampire but at the girl,

studying her face. She was screaming, and he shut that out. He was checking for pain, and she seemed to be terrified but had some slack. If they were going to pull her apart, they hadn't started that yet.

"Hey!" Alex shouted to the girl. "Hey! Don't worry, we're going to get you out of here."

"Shut up," the vampire on the right said, his eyes glistening under the black makeup.

"What's the point of this?" Alex shouted at him. "You're keeping me from the grave? And then what? You bite the little girl anyway?"

The vampire, not the sharpest, seemed to consider. "Just stay back."

Alex held his hands at his sides and glanced at Astrid. They were about twelve feet from the vampires. Beyond lay the grave and the curious digger creature, another fifteen feet back.

"Have to be fast," Alex whispered.

"Right or left?" she answered.

"I'll take the right."

Alex quickly drew his Polibow as he began to run, and he saw the vampire start to pull.

Astrid was in the air, leaping like a gazelle, and she had her staff up, its blade glistening with silver and emerald as she brought it up and back and then down.

The vampires were wide and exposed as they held the girl. Alex hit his vampire square in the forehead and he staggered, brain-dead once more; another bolt in the chest and he was dust. Alex caught the girl just as Astrid landed in the dust cloud that they had created of the two vamps.

Alex looked in the girl's eyes and then pointed at the road, where Sangster was alternating between ushering more parishioners and fighting vampires who were all over the grounds. "You're gonna be okay. Just run for the road."

"But the fires!" the girl cried, looking at the distant curtains and the projection of cities on fire.

"It's not real." Alex crouched and talked to her the way he did his littlest sister. He swept his arm across the vista in the distance. "It's like a TV image on a cloud. When you get to the bottom of the hill, you'll walk right through it."

A voice called, "There!" and Alex quickly stood up.

The strange creature's legs stopped churning, and Alex saw it look up in confusion. Amazing. He could see blood underneath its skin, pumping through it like hydraulic fluid as it stared up at the vampire standing on Allegra Byron's grave marker. It was a male vampire, solidly built with brown hair, his face painted like one of the Queen's minions of death.

"You go after the vamp," Alex told Astrid. "I'll take the leg-churning thing."

"Don't stop!" The vampire pointed down at the ground as he yelled at the creature, whose bug-like eyes blinked. "That's the coffin; just make sure you don't tear it up."

The creature nodded and the legs began to churn once more. Alex had already started running for it.

The creature had broad, humped shoulders and spindly arms, and Alex fired a bolt at it as he got within ten feet. The bolt caught the creature in the shoulder and stuck for a second, hissing before dropping off. It had thick armor all around, probably some kind of augmented, hardened blood, cast with magic in the Scholomance.

Alex leapt on the thing's shoulders and dirt began immediately smacking him in the face. Down below, through the churning legs and soil, Alex could see dark wood, the sturdy edges of the child's coffin.

The creature swiped at him with arms that reminded Alex of the near-useless claws on the sides of a *Tyrannosaurus rex*. He batted them away, holding on to the creature's head, bringing a glass ball out of his go package and smashing it sideways into the holes that he judged to be ears.

The creature howled as holy water gushed through its ear canals, and it stopped digging, whipping its head. Smoke was hissing out of the wound tracks, and Alex saw its teeth, which parted to let a long tongue dart out. The tongue extended and smacked at his chin and Alex grimaced against waves of static. He grabbed the tongue, felt it pulsing in his fingers. Then he jumped off the creature's shoulders, and the creature staggered sideways, crawling out of the hole in pain.

It was on him, then, swiping with its claws at Alex's sides as Alex held the tongue and pumped a bolt into the creature's mouth. He caught it on the cheek. He needed to hit the soft palate of the top of its mouth, to drive a bolt up into its brain.

He saw a flurry of movement out of the corner of his eye as Astrid's staff spun and she landed on a vampire, sending him back against the wall.

On the ground outside the grave now, the creature no longer had to fight with its tiny forearms, and Alex saw the hind legs begin to churn the earth around him. One of the huge hind claws caught the edge of his jacket, sending shreds of cloth flying. Alex kicked at the legs and yelped in pain as the hind claw whacked his leg to the side. *Forget its legs.*

In his peripheral vision, Astrid had the vampire pinned with her staff, and the vampire grabbed Astrid by the front of her jacket and whipped her up, smashing the witch against the wall above him. The vamp dropped around, rising and swiping his long nails at Astrid's neck. Astrid parried the blow. All this in a moment when Alex was bringing his Polibow up again.

Astrid and the vampire were still going at it around the grave when Alex heard a new sound—horses and wheels coming fast.

The creature's mouth was snapping and Alex breathed, aiming his weapon for one of the huge eyes. He felt one of the foreclaws dig into his jacket, scratching at his chest, and Alex quickly pumped a bolt into the creature's eye.

The bolt drove home, deep into the creature's eye socket and into the brain. The creature began to shake, and Alex brought the Polibow down, point-blank at its chest. He fired, sending a bolt into the heart.

In the explosion of dust and ash, Alex felt the heat soften the fibers in his own jacket and melt part of the bandage around his neck. He closed his eyes during the flash lest it melt the contacts to his corneas. Alex quickly got to his feet, searching for Astrid.

She was holding her own, using her staff against the

vampire, but she was evenly matched. Alex brought up his Polibow trying to draw a bead on the vamp, but they kept spinning. He wanted to shout to Astrid to give him room, break off, and let him just shoot the foe.

But suddenly, something grabbed his arm tightly and nearly tore off his hand, and as Alex's arm whipped wild, the Polibow spun away. He was dragged off his feet, his arm threatening to detach from his shoulder, and as he swung around, nearly sliding under a great wooden wheel, he saw Elle, at the reins of a wagon-like coach with a wide bed and several vampires, commanding one of the Queen's skeletal horses.

Alex heard a *fwoosh* sound and looked to see Astrid plunging her staff into her vampire's chest and sending it into oblivion. But Elle was yelling something, and even as Alex untangled himself from her whip, he saw two more vampires, fast and huge, leaping for the grave.

One of them dropped into the grave and had the coffin up in a second, and the other grabbed it, lifting it like something that weighed nothing at all. He was running with it now, and Alex saw Astrid go after him.

The vampire leapt up onto the carriage with the coffin and dropped it into the back, and Elle snapped the reins again. The carriage was beginning to pull out and Alex ran after it. Elle looked back at him, catching his eyes.

"They've got the coffin," Alex said into his Bluetooth. "I'm going after them."

"I'm taking care of this one," Astrid answered, and Alex looked back to see Astrid squaring off with the other vampire, whom Elle had abandoned in order to get away with Allegra's coffin.

"Sangster, what's your situation?" Alex screamed as he ran. A thrill of grave fear rushed through him and Alex set it aside. *Concentrate on what's in front of you.*

Gotta move fast. Alex ran behind the bumping wooden trailer, which was painted in the reddish-brown colors favored by the Scholomance and the new Queen. There were iron bars across either side of the trailer and the coffin was rattling against them. Alex tried to speed up, judging where he would grab a bar. He would have one chance to get on.

He leapt, hitting the top bar and gripping, and then lost it, falling, before grabbing the next bar down. Immediately his body yanked forward, the toes of his shoes dragging and kicking up grass and stones.

The vampire in the back saw Alex now and came forward, reaching for his hand to pull it free, and Alex heaved his body up, getting a leg over the back. The vampire whipped its head and aimed for Alex's shoulder with its teeth.

Alex felt the teeth glancing against his jacket as

he rolled, smashing against the vampire's legs. Alex grabbed the vampire by the feet and pushed upward as he tumbled underneath him, and the creature sailed off the back of the trailer and into the grass.

Alex climbed to his feet, fighting to keep his balance as the carriage barreled past the front of the church and headed for the road.

Up ahead, they were about to hit the edge of the artificial night, and Alex wondered what would happen when they did. Elle whipped the reins and the skeletal horse picked up speed, and then as they reached the wall—

The projection wall pushed back to accommodate them. *Not bad,* Alex thought. Even in this limited demonstration, the spell allowed the Queen's vampires to carry night with them.

They were on a road now, the carriage careening straight down a street where cars zipped around them. Where were they going?

Alex crawled forward and tried to decide what to do. Throw the coffin off the trailer? It would shatter into a thousand pieces. He might even lose the body, the whole point of the operation. He needed to stop the carriage.

Without a Polibow he couldn't shoot. He had a long, dagger-like stake, but he wanted something to throw. He seized a glass ball and threw it at the back of Elle's head.

The jolting carriage killed his shot, the ball slamming into the dashboard of the carriage. Holy water splashed up and hissed against Elle's face and she looked back at him through gritted fangs.

Now the great enclosure of night seemed to stretch out, and Alex saw their path—there was an intersection up ahead, which was in darkness as well, cars suddenly coming into it without lights and swerving. But where were they going?

Alex grabbed the back of the carriage seat, next to Elle, who looked at him and laughed, snapping the reins as they crushed a bicycle, its rider abandoning it as they came near. The skeletal horse clopped over the rear bumper of a small French car and the car swerved off the road, colliding with a mailbox.

"Where are you going?" Alex demanded, holding his stake to the point on Elle's neck just below her ear. She deftly grabbed his wrist and yanked him halfway over the seat.

"What do you care?" He was reading her lips more than hearing her over the cacophony. "You have two days, Alex, before this is what the world looks like."

Beyond the intersection, Alex saw the running water of the Thames, about a hundred yards of it within the dark bubble.

"You can't go to the river," Alex said. "You can't cross running water."

"Why don't you leave the logistics to the professionals?" Elle grabbed his ear and tried to smash Alex against the seat. He struggled to twist free.

Something flashed on the dashboard, and Alex saw what looked like a radar screen, where a large red dot was coming in fast from the right up ahead. Alex heard a long, bellowing horn.

Elle picked up speed, within an eighth of a mile from the intersection. Alex grabbed Elle by the shoulders, reaching his arm around her body, bringing the stake to her neck. "If you're this afraid that we're going to get Allegra's DNA then you must really be worried about us," he said.

"We're taking what's ours."

Right then, Alex made a decision. The red dot on the screen and the sounding horn were probably someone Elle was planning to meet. He could keep trading blows with her until they reached whatever reinforcements were flying down the road up ahead, or he could change the game.

"No, you're not." Alex dropped back and looked at the coffin. Screw it. They could grab what they needed after.

The horn sounded again, and Alex looked over his

shoulder to see an enormous red vehicle like an armored personnel carrier plunge into the intersection, bashing cars out of the way as it slowed.

He looked back at the tiny coffin, all four feet of it, plain and wooden and ancient. "Bye, Elle," he said, and put his fingers under the box's end. With one solid heave, he lifted it and kicked.

The coffin of Allegra Byron tumbled like a bowling pin off the end of the trailer.

Alex felt something heavy collide with his shoulders, Elle's claws grabbing him as she tossed him aside. She was screaming in rage.

The carriage was still moving, out of control and heading into the intersection, as Elle left her seat and pushed past him, reaching out to the wooden casket.

The casket hit the ground and began to roll and shatter, wood splintering. There was no time now. He had to get off and gather it. He looked for a soft landing, found a pickup truck traveling next to them, the driver staring in wonder, and leapt.

Alex hit the metal bed of the pickup truck and felt the driver brake instantly. Alex quickly tucked his shoulders and rolled into the front of the pickup bed. He got to his feet, looking out onto the road and wincing as the coffin continued to pinwheel, its top flying off and its sides exploding. Pieces of it smashed into an oncoming car.

Alex dropped out of the truck to the side of the road, wincing in guilt as he prepared for the grand finale of a tiny mummified body flying through someone's windshield.

But that didn't happen at all. The coffin of Lord Byron's daughter burst open like an old tomato and spat out a flurry of paper, straw, fluttering yellow ribbons, and cobblestones.

Alex got out of the way of another vehicle and stood on the curb in shock, looking back to see Elle, who dropped to her knees in her wild carriage, arms outstretched toward the coffin, her black-painted eyes wide with rage.

The carriage swept into the intersection and smashed into the enormous red vehicle, and the last Alex saw of Elle, her body was catapulted through the air into the open side of the personnel carrier as it zoomed past. She disappeared into it completely, leaving the bones of her horse.

The carrier sped away, and Alex could still hear her screaming as he brought his eyes back to the obliterated, empty coffin.

Chapter 20

The coffin is empty. Alex ran into the street, daylight already streaming back in, the nightmare of darkness lifted. He held out his hands toward traffic in vain hope that this would somehow keep cars from running over him. "Astrid, help me get the pieces!" he called into his wireless.

Get the pieces. He wouldn't think about it until he recovered the pieces. Alex ran around, grabbing wood and tossing it to the side of the road. He ran after bits of straw and shredded paper that turned to dust in the damp air. Amazingly, at least one motorist hopped out of his car and helped him, and then Astrid was there, running, too.

At the side of the road Alex had a stack of ruined casket—lid and bottom, pieces of all six sides, and the stuffing, a few bits of which he shoved into his pack.

Something caught his eye, and Alex squinted, feeling his contacts swim as his eyelids squeezed his eyeballs, trying to drag a few extra feet of vision out of them. What looked to him like a paper flag was stuck in a corner of the casket, flitting in the wind against the opposite curb. Alex ran, dodging cars and delivery trucks, and when he reached the chunk of wood he saw that the paper was an envelope. There was a plug of wax on the back with a stamped indicia that looked to Alex like an early version of the one he saw every day: *P*, and below it: *Talia sunt.*

In the coffin of Allegra Byron, he had found a letter from Dr. John Polidori himself.

Alex picked it up and looked back across the street at Astrid, who stood with the other chunks of wood. He waved it.

"What's that?" he heard her say.

"I think it's a letter." That was all there was. He turned it over in his hand—very thin and delicate, with a wax stamp on the back and a pressed, ornate letter *P*. He tapped his Bluetooth. "Sangster, we found—"

Alex suddenly heard sirens ringing out. "Sangster, where are you?"

A click finally responded in his ear. "Alex, are you hurt?" Sangster said with urgency.

Alex was running back to the churchyard, waving at Astrid to follow. He ran back around the street, huffing as he made his way down the sidewalk. An ambulance was pulling to the curb next to the Polidorium van.

Sangster was walking next to the gurney that two English paramedics were putting Armstrong on. Alex and Astrid met them as they were moving across the lawn.

"What is it? Is she—?"

"Don't be so dramatic," Armstrong screamed. She was lying on the gurney as the paramedics moved her quickly, trying to put an oxygen mask on her face. She tried to grab at her knee, which was bleeding profusely, and the paramedics were fighting with her. "This is not necessary; I have a van," he heard her say.

Sangster was bleeding from a wound in his shoulder, and he spoke rapidly to Alex in short spurts. "I'm fine, leave it," he said as he waved off a medic. "There were reinforcements among the skulls; they wanted to keep us away from the grave. One of them caught Anne's leg as she kicked him and bit into her knee. Did they get the body?"

"What about Armstrong?" Alex asked as she was whisked into the ambulance. She was shouting muffled profanities at them as the ambulance doors closed.

"Just a cluster—it happens all the time. Someone must have called the EMS, and they're not gonna take no for an answer. It's fine; they'll get her checked in, and we'll have someone kidnap her tonight and bring her back to the farmhouse." Again he said: "Alex, did they get the body?"

Alex made an open, helpless gesture with his hands. "There was no body. It was empty."

"What?!" Sangster's question sounded as angry as it did shocked.

"The Scholomance looked as surprised as we were. Elle screamed bloody murder. But I did get something . . . I don't know; it's a letter."

Sangster shook his head and doubled over for a second, breathing as he put his hands on his knees. Sangster stood up, as if beating back his stress with a poker. He turned and started to jog toward the Polidorium van. "We gotta go."

Alex and Astrid looked at each other and followed when Alex repeated, "I got a letter here!" The ambulance was pulling away, its siren wailing.

Sangster stopped at the door to the van and turned back. "What?"

"Well, like I said, the coffin was empty. But I got a letter here that fell out of it. No DNA, but we got the ribbons and stones that weighed it all down, and we got a letter." He waved it idiotically, standing next to the open van door as the engine idled. "It's from Polidori."

"So open it," Astrid said.

Alex looked at Sangster. "Maybe we should take it to the lab first."

Sangster shook his head. "What does it say?"

Alex tore into the old paper, feeling it splinter in his hands.

There was a battered and stained sheet of paper within. He sighed at the few words written there. "The coarsest sensations of men." Alex paused, then shook his head. "Everybody get that? No body, but we got 'the coarsest sensations of men.' Why? Because nothing can ever be easy."

Sangster turned around and ran his hands along the roof of the van, as if answers would be found in the steel. "The coarsest sensations . . . ?"

"The coarsest sensations of men."

"Right," Sangster said, pressing his forehead against the van.

"It sounds like a pirate thing."

Sangster swore and smacked the van with his fist.

"What?" Alex said.

"It's a line from *Frankenstein*."

CHAPTER 21

"Alex, we're out of time." Director Carreras, a paunchy, middle-aged man with a Spanish name and a British accent, spoke the words flatly, as if to end an argument they had barely begun.

Alex realized the moment he, Sangster, and Astrid slunk into the Polidorium headquarters below the woods surrounding Lake Geneva that the game was considered over. There were twice as many agents as usual in the halls, and when Sangster had driven their van in from the airstrip, they had been slowed by heavy traffic moving down through the tunnels. There were rocket launchers being prepared. He saw agents practicing formations and assaults in fake urban landscapes in the far corners of the cavern.

And then Sangster had been texted and ordered immediately to a briefing room, and Alex and Astrid were sent to see the principal. Or in this case, the director. Armstrong was with him, a pair of crutches leaning against the wall behind her. She looked sour.

"What do you mean, 'out of time'?" Alex said. "We have two more days. Two days to make a weapon that can stop the Queen."

"With what? The DNA is gone," Carreras said. "The one shot was to find DNA from Claire and Byron's daughter, and we've missed it."

"Well, don't you think that's a little strange?" Alex said. He waved the envelope. "This is a letter. From Polidori, from *your founder*. It's a clue. Sangster said it has something to do with *Frankenstein*."

Carreras sighed. He had been the one to give Sangster permission to bring Alex into the Polidorium in the first place. He even seemed to know Alex's dad, and Alex was aware that he truly owed every part of his adventures with the group to him. But the director had run out of patience. "A clue, if it's real, left nearly two hundred years ago. Agent Van Helsing, we have preparations to make. We've run out of time to chase a cure. I've already assigned Agent Sangster to more pressing matters. This mission is done."

"Sir, Astrid and I are still on the search."

"That is not the plan."

"So what—" He looked around the boardroom at Armstrong, then at Astrid, who sat silently. "What is your plan?"

Carreras tapped a keyboard and brought up a map onscreen—Europe, then it toggled and unfolded to show the western hemisphere. Little gray lights blinked all across the map. "We have to prepare for the next phase."

"Next phase?" That didn't sound good.

"Everyone has a job, Alex," Carreras said. "Agent Sangster is assigned to France, where the Polidorium will rally with the French secret police. All of the high-ranking agents are being field-promoted to Special Agents in Charge and are now receiving their orders. Transports are leaving on the hour. These gray lights you see? Those are Polidorium stations. In ten minutes I have a conference call with the defense authorities of every nation. U.N. peacekeeping forces are being shifted and reassigned."

Alex looked at the map. Switzerland. France. Germany. The U.K. The U.S. Russia. He shook his head. "This is giving up."

Carreras looked at Alex. "No. This is defense. The

Scholomance is not negotiating, Alex. They're not asking for a ransom. They're going to plunge the world into darkness, and we have to be ready for a new . . . normal."

"And what is the new normal?"

"There will be armies of vampires in the streets," Armstrong said. "Chatter among the clans is off the charts. They're preparing to occupy every major city when there's no more daylight. We'll need armed forces on every street corner. We'll need to close schools for a time until we can figure out how to get them open— if we can. Hospitals, don't even get me started. Forget shopping malls. Forget grocery stores. We'll have to have armed forces delivering food to protected drop zones, and escort civilians in groups from their neighborhoods to the storehouses."

"Something like this," Carreras cut in, "was bound to happen. We always knew it and we have the plans in place."

Alex pushed back his hair, friendly faces the world over zipping through his brain. "I haven't seen anything about this . . . on the news." Even though he hadn't actually been watching the news, he knew what he was saying was stupid. If people knew this was coming they'd have taken to the streets already. "Are you going to tell everyone . . . to prepare them?"

"We're not announcing it until the night before, until late Sunday night. There wouldn't be any point. By the time we make the announcement, roadblocks will be in place."

Alex understood what Carreras was saying. Give the people of the world a few more days of thinking everything was going to keep on the way it had kept on their whole lives. Monday would bring a new order, when every family would be prisoners in their own home.

"And not just vampires," Carreras continued. "Every kind of vampire the Scholomance wants to roll out. According to Sangster, they had a Nuckelavee digging up the grave in London."

"A what?" Alex asked. Then he remembered. The thing with the roving legs was a Nuckelavee. He had seen one of them at Creature School, in fact. He waved this away, trying again. "Look, I can find the DNA. I have the instructions for the vial gun. I just need the DNA. We don't have to assume that the apocalypse is coming."

"And again I ask you," Carreras repeated, "find it with what? Find it where?"

Alex sat back, drummed his fingers on the table. He pointed at Astrid. "What about Hexen?"

"I checked in," Astrid said. "We are prepared to

cooperate. We feel a certain responsibility for Queen Claire."

Alex shook his head. "So I guess you're going back to . . ."

"The Orchard?" Astrid asked. "I could, but I have an assignment I'm still on, so those are not my orders."

"Oh, right." Alex turned to the rest of them. "Did I mention this? She's a spy here to watch *me*."

Carreras blinked. "I think under the circumstances you can use the help."

"Oh? Where am *I* supposed to go?"

"We've left this up to you, Alex. You were Sangster's protégé, so if you choose to stay on at this time, we can use you with him in France, or you can choose your current station, Geneva. You'd be reporting to an agent named Hall. Or you can go back to school, since you have that right. Or we're prepared to send you home. You can leave within the hour. Wyoming might need you. Personally I think with the population involved, we could use you here more, but again, it's up to you."

For a moment Alex pictured it, his parents' house in Wyoming. They would have Dad, who had all his skills, and Mom, who had all of Astrid's and more. And they would have two teenage girls and two smaller girls. And it would be dark outside, with roving bands of vampires led by whoever ruled that part of North America.

"No, no, this is crazy," Alex said, shaking his head. "I don't accept this."

"We are *out*," Carreras repeated slowly, "of time."

Alex scanned all the faces. He was done arguing. New plan. "How long do I have to decide?"

"Twenty minutes." Carreras stood. He seemed to slump for a moment, then stood straighter, smoothing his suit coat over his paunch. "After this meeting, I'm afraid things will be such that you won't see me like this anymore. Agent Van Helsing, it has been good working with you." He extended a hand.

Alex shook it. "I'll be in the library."

As Alex walked out he looked at Astrid. "You gonna follow at a distance or just come on?"

In the Polidorium library, an enormous room of plain-gray metal shelves and high white ceilings, the first thing Alex grabbed was a Polidorium tablet with an internet connection.

"What are you doing?" Astrid asked as they took a table in the back.

"Get me a copy of *Frankenstein*." Alex booted up the tablet as his mind raced through what he had learned about the book just a month or so before. "Both editions, 1818 and 1831."

"What are you looking for?"

Alex removed his wireless and clicked it off, and gestured for Astrid to do the same. "John Polidori had Mary Shelley put clues about Claire and Byron in *Frankenstein*. I'm hoping there's more."

"What are you doing, Alex?" Astrid shook her head. "They said you can go home. They've given up on this. In fact, I think you said you were out, that you didn't want to do this anymore."

"Go home to what? Everlasting night because they don't want to *read*? No, no. Just . . . get the books; we quit later."

She shrugged. "*I* never wanted to quit anything."

Alex pointed, not looking up as he scribbled notes. "Books."

By the time she returned with the books, Alex had opened an internet chat and in a separate window entered the phrase *the coarsest sensations of men* into Google. The search brought up the notation instantly. "Sangster was right: It *is* a phrase from *Frankenstein*." For a moment Alex wondered at someone's ability to hear a few words and place the book from which they came. He had internet tools to do this, but only careful reading over time could allow you to do it by memory. He had the suspicion that he could pick any five words out of any book Sangster had read and the teacher would be able to nail it. He could use him now.

A voice spoke from the tablet, young and female. "Are you sure you need this?"

Alex whispered near a microphone grating at the corner of the tablet. "Yes. Do you still have access to the forms?"

There was the sound of typing. The voice on the other end was looking something up. "Yes."

Astrid looked at the chat window and read the name of Alex's chat partner. "Who are you talking to? Who is 'RVH'?"

"That would be Ronnie Van Helsing," Alex said. "Short for Veronica. My little sister."

"Where is she?"

"In the States, but she's the only one who can do what I need her to do in the time we have." Alex scribbled some notes on a sheet of paper.

"New girlfriend, Al?" the voice taunted.

"Not the time, Ron," Alex answered. "Just set me up and come back when you do." He took the book Astrid handed him and flipped through the 1818 edition of *Frankenstein*, to the place where his Google search had led him, chapter 11. He looked at Astrid. "Polidori had Shelley put her hints in the 1831 edition, but here this phrase is in the 1818 version. That means it *wasn't* a plant by Polidori; it was just a reference. Still, see if there's a difference in the 1831 book."

Astrid flipped to chapter 11 and frowned. "It's not here."

"The chapters are different." Alex glanced back at the internet version. "Try chapter . . . nineteen in yours."

"Okay." Astrid searched the pages. "Paragraph?"

"A few pages in, starts 'On the whole island, there were but three miserable huts.'"

Astrid found it and they pushed the books together and confirmed that the paragraphs were the same in both, just in different chapters. Alex made a decision that the difference meant nothing. He had to move quickly and rely on snap decisions.

"What's going on in this section?" Astrid asked.

Alex scanned, relying as much on having read the book recently as on what he was seeing. "Uh, Dr. Frankenstein has been threatened, and he has to build a bride for the monster. He has to go off by himself to do it. And he chooses an island." He paused and looked up. "Is it possible that Polidori hid Allegra's body away on this island, wherever it is—this is somewhere in Scotland, by the way—and used a reference to *Frankenstein* to lead us there?"

"Why would Polidori do that?"

"I guess to keep the body safe."

"But why not just leave instructions?"

"If I had to guess? Because he didn't want random grave robbers to know, and because from my limited experience, that's kind of the way he worked."

"It's a lot of assumptions, Alex."

"Yes," Alex hissed, "but look: Every clue we've followed so far has been *right*. The vampires caught up to us at Harrow. We were right. So this has a good shot at being right, too."

Astrid sighed and looked at the paragraph. "This island is in Scotland?"

Alex read some. "They don't name it. Ugh. So it's just 'an island.' In the Orkneys," he read, jumping around paragraphs. He went back to the computer and brought up the Orkneys on the internet, finding a map of tiny islands scattered around the north of Scotland. "The Orkneys is an archipelago, a system of islands. We can't search a system of islands for a two-hundred-year-old body. Not in the time we have." *Need a new plan.*

"How would you search?"

"Hang on, hang on; don't get ahead of me. I know

you're good at that, but don't do that right now." He gave her a half-smile and turned back to reading. "Orkneys. What does Mary Shelley say in the book? Frankenstein gets food from the mainland, which is five miles distant." Then he looked at his watch. "Okay. 'Five miles from the mainland.' That could be any of *these*, along the south of the archipelago. And it doesn't make sense that Polidori would leave a clue that could point to *anything*. By the way, I think we've got ten minutes and then our friends come looking for us."

Next he brought up a list of the individual Orkney Islands. "Oh," he said.

"What?"

"It's not 'an island five miles off the mainland of Scotland.' It's 'five miles off Mainland,' which is the name of another island. I hope, I mean. There is one called Mainland."

"Go with your gut, Alex," Astrid said.

"If this"—and now he pointed at the largest island in the group—"is Mainland, then there's only one island on this map that's within five miles." He spun the tablet around to show it to her.

Astrid read the name. "Brough of Birsay?"

"Brough of Birsay. An isolated, desolate island of old ruins. *That's* where Mary Shelley picked to be the lab for

Frankenstein building the bride. And it's where Polidori picked to hide the body of Allegra Byron when he stole it, or most likely bribed it, off the gravediggers in England." There was something else, though. Something Armstrong had said.

"Nuckelavee," Alex said. When Astrid looked at him, he continued, "That digger creature the Scholomance brought. I learned about them at Creature School. It's Scottish. It's *also* from here, from the Orkney Islands."

Astrid shook her head. "That seems like a strange coincidence, that they'd use a creature from the place where the DNA is actually buried."

"It's the other way around," Alex said. "The Scholomance really seemed to think that they were going to find the body in England. You know what it means? That Polidori moved the body to the island because he knew that would be the place where Claire would set off the Triumph of Death. He knew the spell would be set off there, and he wanted to plant us a weapon."

"Something else, though," Astrid said. "That implies that the Strangers—Blacktowers—have been continuing Polidori's preparations. Outside the Polidorium."

"Or Polidori was working for Blacktowers," Alex offered.

"Does that matter?"

"It might if I ever get the chance to ask Blacktowers."

Ronnie's voice spoke up, interrupting them. "Alex, give them eight minutes."

"Thanks. Hang up now and erase all of this." He looked at his watch. Time was about up in the library. He stood, closing the tablet and shoving it into his go package. He headed out of the library, saying, "Come on. If we're right, we could stop Claire at the Brough of Birsay."

The moment they stepped out of the library's glass door into the hall, an alarm bell rang.

"What's that?" Astrid asked.

"I just removed a Polidorium tablet computer with all of the database and more from its home area." He was walking faster now, then jogging as the alarm receded behind them. "Another few moments and it'll go off throughout the farmhouse."

"Then what?" They swiftly walked past a couple of agents around the next corner, who paid them no mind because they were watching a training video on the wall about how to defend a grocery store.

"We won't be here then." Alex clicked on his wireless and instantly heard a chirp.

"Alex, where are you?" Carreras yelled.

"I've thought about it, sir." They reached the carpeted

hallway that led to the main hangar, and Alex made note of the muddy tracks where countless agents had been coming and going. Custodianship was getting lax. He opened the door for Astrid and they were in the hangar, running down the metal steps. He scanned the area, looking at pilots working on their planes and maintenance crews at the vans. He whispered to Astrid, "Do you have a spell for opening doors?"

"Yes."

"Good." He made a beeline for the motorcycles and picked one. It was Sangster's black Triumph.

Alex started the engine as Astrid hopped on, and this time they attracted the attention of a couple of the agents.

Carreras came back. "So? You thought about it?"

"I can't stay," Alex said. "Good luck."

"Alex, what do you mean? Are you going home or to the school or what?"

Alex started to roll the bike, past the other parked motorcycles, and then they were cruising past a maintenance crew working on a Bradley Fighting Vehicle.

"Good luck, sir."

Alarm bells erupted as the time for a negligent agent to return the tablet to the library lapsed and a full theft was assumed. Now Alex saw cameras in the hangar swivel and point at him as he throttled the Triumph and picked up speed, heading to the start of the exit ramp. It was half a mile to the surface.

"Hey!" shouted a guard near the entrance. "Stop!"

Alex saluted as Astrid held on and they began to move up the ramp, which was wide enough for a pair of tanks. He saw gun emplacements swiveling and he watched the cameras. Surely they wouldn't shoot him. Right?

"Where are you going, Alex?" the voice sounded in his helmet.

"If you pay attention, you'll know."

"Alex!" called Astrid. He could barely hear her over the roar of the engine. "Why not just throw the tablet away?"

"Because I *want* them to know!" he shouted. "They're giving up and I want them to know!" Alex pointed up ahead, where a closed garage door about a half mile away slowly grew larger. "Can you open that door?" He looked over his shoulder at Astrid. "Like now?"

Astrid brought up her staff and reached it around him. She screamed something he didn't understand. Now he heard the sounds of other engines behind them. There was a flash from the end of her staff, and Alex saw the door warp for a second. She called again, something with thick consonants that he couldn't make out, and then he heard, *"Open."*

The door swung open an inch or two and they were still zooming toward it. "It's protected against magic."

"I'm not stopping, do you hear me, sir? I'm not stopping."

The British voice sounded curious. "Oh? Where are you going?"

"Scotland. Are you going to stop me because you don't want me stealing a computer?"

"Just turn around and we'll talk about it."

"Talk about it? I am doing *your job*, sir!" Alex called. "Are you people insane? You're falling back to babysitting a vampire apocalypse? *No.*"

Alex looked back at the line of motorcycles and a truck behind him. An agent was hanging out of the side of the truck with a machine gun.

"I am going to hit this door at sixty miles an hour," said Alex. "And I'm gonna be jelly, but you know what? *You'll* have a door to fix, and your defenses will be damaged, and you'll have vampires coming in your front door under permanent nightfall."

The door was looming. Alex sped up.

"You won't get far, Alex," came the response, and the door swung open, heavy and fast, and he burst through the exit into the night and the woods.

The motorcycles followed him as he shot through the trees, keeping their distance, watching. "They have no idea what we're doing," Alex said.

"I hope *you* know what you're doing," Astrid shouted.

Alex veered around a tree and zipped onto the road to Secheron village. After a moment he heard a new sound, a helicopter zooming in overhead. A searchlight opened up and surrounded them, so they cast a long shadow on the road.

"You want me to take out the helicopter, maybe damage it a little?"

Alex waved his arm. "No! For Pete's sake, there's no such thing as damaging a helicopter a little. And besides, *that's* not the Polidorium." He looked back and saw that his Polidorium escorts were still behind him, though. Alex waved at the helicopter, signaling *Up ahead and left*.

Alex headed another quarter mile up the road, and then veered off near a clearing, a soccer field. With a loud, chutting sound of rotor blades, the helicopter chased past them and then swiveled in the field, dropping down and hanging a few inches off the deck.

"Okay." Alex ground the bike to a halt and hopped off, tossing his helmet. "Come on."

"Whose helicopter is that?" They were running across the field now.

As they drew closer, Alex saw a huge red cross on the side of the chopper and the blazing words BRINGING HEALTH AND KNOWLEDGE TO THE WORLD.

The pilot, whom Alex didn't know, waved at him and Astrid as they scrambled into the side door of the chopper.

Alex and Astrid sprawled on the inside of the chopper and were still getting into their seats as they lifted off the soccer field and into the air, a stream of motorcycles and vehicles following. Alex waved at them as they went.

As the chopper pitched and they put on their seat belts, the waters of Lake Geneva sparkled and zipped by below them.

Alex pulled a headset off the wall and spoke to the pilot. "Thanks very much."

"No problem," came the voice of the pilot. "So you have humanitarian work to do in the middle of the night?"

"We have an early morning." Astrid was clearly full of questions, and Alex held up a finger to stall her for a moment. He asked the pilot, "How long till we get there?"

"Three hours. That's why the dispatcher ordered a long-distance unit. Were those guys *chasing* you?"

"Don't worry about it," Alex answered. "Thanks again." He put the headset away and turned to Astrid. "I called the States and had my sister Ronnie fake a work order. If anyone asks, we're doing a humanitarian visit on the Brough of Birsay. That's what we do."

"Who?"

Alex tapped a plaque on the wall above the window of the chopper as they crossed over the other side of the lake, and the trees and land of France came into view. In a little while, they would be over the ocean.

The plaque read:

THE VAN HELSING FOUNDATION.

CHAPTER 22

It was a cold, gray dawn, and the helicopter bearing Astrid and Alex came to the Brough of Birsay, a desolate green island barely an eighth of a mile long.

As they neared, Alex's eyes flickered open and he took in the island, where the Atlantic churned against rocky beaches and ancient ruins, and one structure was visible from miles away. "That's the lighthouse," the pilot yelled back to them. "Do you want me to put you there?"

The lighthouse, not as tall as the lighthouses on the eastern seaboard of the United States but very similar in its white wood and squat adjacent building, sat on the north shore, across the island from where they would be coming over land.

Alex blinked several times, coming awake from having allowed himself a couple of hours of sleep. "Hey." He tapped Astrid's shoulder. "We're here."

The young witch opened her eyes and stretched, looking out at the island.

Alex was watching the water around the island and then shouted to the pilot, "Wait, wait, hang back. Uh, keep your distance while we . . . decide."

"What is it?" Astrid asked.

He had to raise his voice some for her to hear him. "This is Birsay. The Vikings called it *Byrgisay*, the fortress island. They built strongholds here, but as you can see most of those are ruins." He swept his arm out across the island.

"You've been reading," she said, just as loudly.

"Just a little after you fell asleep." Alex was scanning the island, then realized he was looking for a hut or house like Mary Shelley described in the book, but of course that was absurd. He saw ruins scattered across the island, old stone foundations of Norse houses and churches. He had no idea where they would begin to look, but they could probably cover the whole island in an hour or less.

There was another angle he was considering as the chopper pitched eastward into the sun, staying away from the island and running parallel to the scrubby beaches.

"Where is Claire going to be?" he asked aloud. "If the Queen is going to set off her big Triumph, where is she going to do it?"

Astrid looked out. "If I had to pick, I'd go with the oldest ruins."

Alex pointed to one end of the island. He saw a jumble of ruins, including a *broch*, a fortification of stones built by the Picts, ancient peoples who held the island until the Vikings drove them off. There were Christian and Viking ruins as well. "That all looks old."

Astrid shivered, and Alex watched her eyes take in the whole island as she looked out the window next to him. "Yeah, there's magic there, but there's magic all over here; if feels like . . . Rome."

"Ley lines?"

She nodded. "Magic real estate."

"Yeah," said Alex. He was eager to get a look at the ruins. But they also needed to set up their own HQ. He was about to tell the pilot to set them at the lighthouse when he looked down to the water, the gray foam churning with the heavy wind, and the chopper pitched and steadied. The long, dark shadow of a coral reef curved along below the surface. A rumble of static passed through Alex's mind and he leaned forward instinctively.

"Follow the reef," he told the pilot, and the chopper continued the curve around the island.

Alex felt it still, and he looked at Astrid. "They're here already. Hiding among the coral."

An abrupt growl in his mind shocked him back an inch.

This was cold water, and cold-water islands don't have coral.

Water was burbling next to the dark shadow, the not-coral.

"Turn back. Turn back now!" Alex called, and the pilot threw him a look.

"What?"

"Turn back! Head to Mainland! *Now!*"

But there was a growling in his mind and something bursting from the water, and then the helicopter pitched violently as a chunk of ice the size of a football slammed into the side of the chopper. Alex looked out.

An icy shape like a gun emplacement had risen from the waves and turned toward them, the ice folding in on itself and forming something like a cannon. Alex saw it spasm once, and then another white ball was flying toward them.

The chopper spun for a moment and the pilot fought with it. "Someone's shooting at us. What the hell is that?" the pilot screamed.

"Move out farther, a quarter mile; we have to bail out." Alex was up and ripping through panels in the back, searching for gear. He set a flare gun aside and found a life raft. He prayed whoever was shooting from the water would have limited vision if they got farther away. "You can go, but we have to bail. Does this raft have CO_2?"

"You're crazy!" the pilot called, and then cursed as the ice slammed into them again. "We're going back to Mainland."

Alex glanced at Astrid as he threw the door open, looking down at the water. They were fifty feet off the ground.

"Take us lower, take us lower," he said, and the pilot turned, zipping across the water as the ice gun discharged again, in the distance, too far to connect. "If we're lucky they'll think we went away. No way they know it's us; this is just them holding everyone at bay while they get ready."

"What are we doing?" Astrid asked, joining him at the open door.

"We can make that." Alex judged the distance, which

had dropped to thirty feet.

He held the rubber raft out the door and shook it, letting it roll out and float limply behind the chopper. "On my mark, we're going to jump. Pilot, then you're clear. Tell no one. No one!"

Astrid looked back toward the island. "Won't they see us?"

"If so, we'll have a lot less rowing to do," Alex said. "I'm going."

Alex breathed, then pulled the cord. He couldn't hear the minor explosion as the raft filled with air, and he put his hands on the top ropes as Astrid did the same. The raft was about six feet wide and perfectly round. "Keep your hands on the ropes and land on the raft. It might turn over, it probably *will* turn over, so when it does, just swim out from under it, and we'll turn it back over together. Don't let go of the ropes."

She was looking down. "Uh . . ."

"Listen," Alex said, channeling Sangster. "We don't live in a world where nothing goes wrong. We live in a world where we have a plan when it does. Okay? Now go."

Another lob of ice flew in the distance, and Alex and Astrid leapt with the raft.

There was a half second of air until Alex felt the wind

get smashed out of his lungs as the raft hit the waves, and he and Astrid both cried out involuntarily. They slammed against one another, and the waves caught the raft. Alex scrambled to stay on top of it, but they were caught in a wave and it tipped them over.

Freezing water shot through Alex's clothes as he found himself under the raft, sinking and holding on to the ropes. He held out his hand and felt Astrid, and kicked, moving back until he found the surface outside the side of the raft. After a moment she came up as well.

The chopper was zipping off in the distance, and Alex hoped that there were no eyes looking out on the water to see them ditch. The gun emplacement hurled a few more ice chunks at the retreating chopper, and he judged that they had not seen him.

As they hung there in the water, Alex's teeth were chattering, and he said, "We have to turn it over. Then we paddle it to shore."

Astrid nodded rapidly, barely able to move her face. They each went to opposite ends of the raft and widened their arms. He felt the cold leaching his strength. "Pull this side, hard, on three," he said, indicating his right. "One," and he bounced in the air, "two," and she did the same, "three."

They plunged hard on the edge, pulling the ropes

and lifting with their other arms, and the raft strained against them. Alex felt his toes going numb as the raft swayed on its edge, and then finally fell back. "We get in at the same time, you on that side, me on this side," Alex said. "Throw your leg up."

She copied his moves and they crawled up, icy water tugging at them.

Finally they lay in the raft, exhausted, looking into the sunrise, freezing water pooling around their bodies.

Exhaustion crept over Alex, his body shaking, his knees wanting to curl up. He pressed his forehead against Astrid's for a second and they lay there, shaking.

Needing to keep going, Alex forced his chattering teeth apart and spoke. "This thing has paddles. Let's go."

CHAPTER 23

The emergency hut on the Brough of Birsay was a government-maintained cabin attached to the lighthouse, and as Alex broke in, his body numb with cold, it seemed to him the most wonderful place he had ever seen. The hut was simple and unassuming, with cheap plastic furniture and linoleum tile, but it had a fireplace and kitchenette and even first aid supplies, rendering it perfect. It would make a good headquarters to begin their search for the remains of Allegra Byron. Somewhere on this island, John Polidori had secreted away a body. They had a day to find it.

Wearing one of the dirty pairs of overalls he had liberated for himself and for Astrid from a supply closet, he surveyed their tools. They had laid out the material from Astrid's bag and Alex's go package on a countertop in the small building adjacent to the lighthouse. A fire crackled in the fireplace now, where some of their clothes hung drying, and he hoped that the vampires surrounding the island did not have sentries out to see the smoke of the fire.

Astrid was chanting over a nearby table, rolling wax paper—also from the kitchenette—into small cartridges with each incantation. "How many can you make?" Alex asked.

"I can do about ten push-backs," she said. "That will stagger someone back, knock them off balance. If we were facing humans I could make about three heart-stoppers; those are costly. But our foes don't have beating hearts. I have my staff, which is silver, wood, and enchanted metal. I can do about four fireballs."

"Those will help." Alex stacked Polibow cartridges as he counted them. "I have four cartridges of sixteen bolts, eight glass balls." Finally he set down the vial gun, which was open and empty, waiting for a vial of whatever agent he could place in it. Next to this were the two vials, each one half-full of holy water, still waiting for the active ingredient. "I should have raided the armory when I had the chance."

She looked up, smiling at his disappointment. "When? When you were stealing the computer or when you were trying to talk them into opening up the door?"

He smiled back at her and nodded. "I suppose you're right. Anyway, I don't think having a machine gun is what will make a difference. Okay. We have our weapons. Any minute now we'll have our clothes." He padded over to the fire in his bare feet and felt at his jacket, shirt, and pants. They were still damp. Out the window, the Atlantic Ocean pounded against the rocky cliff beyond the lighthouse, and a thick fog lay over the land. "I don't feel any static. I think they were watching for air traffic, but they're lying in wait now."

He sat down in the blanket on one of the plastic chairs, leaning his shoulder against the table. "Do you think I'm crazy?" he asked her.

Astrid looked up from rolling her spells, stopping the chant she had just started. "Why?"

A teakettle sounded, and Alex started, and realized he was still jumpy. What he needed was more sleep, but there wasn't time for that. The nap on the chopper would have to do. He went over to the stove and poured himself and Astrid a cup of tea with a couple of the tea bags he had found in the cabinets. "The Polidorium is already prepared for the next step. They've given up completely. And I have to admit, I'm not sure how we're going to find this body, either."

Alex carried back the two cups of tea, placing them on the table. "So, am I? Crazy, I mean?"

"You know what you are?" Astrid joined him. "You're a person who doesn't give up. You can fight when it's all done, but as long as there's still a chance, you're going to keep working on it. You're Mad Meg."

He nodded. "Okay, so now that we've established that it's all okay because I'm a lot like your crazy Dutch aunt," Alex said, "you tell me: How do we find this body? We don't have a scanner, and I don't think one would work, anyway. This island has a lot of old stone ruins, but none of the peasant huts that Mary Shelley described or that Polidori might have used. So what do we do?"

Astrid thought a moment. "If we had something of Allegra's it would be easier."

Alex shrugged. Then Astrid leaned forward, draping her blanketed arm over his shoulder. He felt her fingers behind his ear. "What's this?"

Alex was laughing in spite of himself. "What are you doing, finding a quarter?"

She drew back, twisting a piece of black wood in her fingers, wrapped in a bit of yellow ribbon. "This is a piece of Allegra's coffin," she said. "And the ribbon is a piece of the ones that held the stones in place to weigh it down. I made a bet that the ribbon belonged to her. I guess we can find out."

Astrid took Alex's teacup, set it on the counter with her own, and turned back to the table. There was a salt and pepper set, and she grabbed the pepper and set it on the counter as well, leaving just the salt.

"What are you doing?"

"Working." Satisfied with the saltshaker alone on the table, Astrid went to the kitchenette and rummaged around. She brought back a bowl and dropped the chunk of wood in it. She looked around, grabbed Alex's teacup, tossed the tea into the bowl, and began grinding the moist wood.

"Is there anything I can—"

"You can check the dryer." By which she meant the clothes in front of the fireplace.

Astrid was muttering to herself as she ground the wood and then she stopped, taking a knife from a drawer. Alex was about to protest when she cut herself on the finger, but he kept his mouth shut.

Astrid squeezed a few drops of blood into the bowl and then ground on, and he noticed she kept her cut finger splayed out a little, favoring it. "Nothing in magic is free," she said. "It costs in soul or in blood."

When she was done, she walked over to the table with the bowl, and daubed her fingers in the mash of wood and blood. She began to smear it on the table, creating a circle.

"Mother Gretel, your daughter calls out to you," Astrid whispered, and then she slipped farther into words that Alex did not recognize.

The saltshaker began to quiver on the table.

"Show us the home of this spirit, show us her place."

The saltshaker began to move, all on its own, traveling around the edge of the smear, which Alex presumed was an outline of the island. It stopped, shaking, quivering along the water, nearly tipping over as it began to spin. Alex thought it would explode right there, and then it shot into the smear, about a third of the way in.

Astrid indicated its position. "Check that against the map."

"That's incredible," Alex said. "I've never seen anything like that." He picked up the Polidorium tablet and showed her the Google World map of the Brough of Birsay. "That's near the old English church—ruins of stones that we saw from the air."

He got up and rummaged around in the kitchen, continuing, "It's a circle made up of granite stones. Maybe

Polidori buried her near the stones. It *would* make it easier to find."

Astrid seemed pleased. "What are you getting?"

"Something for your grievous wound." Alex returned to the table and took her hand, looking at the cut. He tore open the Band-Aid he had retrieved and put it over the end of her finger.

Astrid's eyes seemed to sparkle as she trilled her fingers. "Well, thank you."

"So . . ." Alex took his hands away and started to drum his fingers on the table, stopping instantly. He got up. "So let's go. We've got a body to find."

CHAPTER 24

The Pictish stones of the Brough of Birsay stood guard over a patch of green earth fifty feet wide, and Astrid and Alex wandered through hurriedly after hiking across the fifty-acre island. Every few minutes, one or the other of them would stop to look out at the water and the dark shadow offshore, wondering if they would be discovered. They stopped in the middle of the graveyard—barely observable as it was, just a series of rectangles of worn low stones. A high Pictish slab stood at one end, before three long strips of stone in the grass.

There was a ruined church nearby, roofless and mostly destroyed, its walls made of flat stones. That was a more recent building, but even it would have lain in ruins when Polidori was here. Alex was lost again.

He threw Astrid a dismayed look. "All I see here are ancient stones. Is there any way we can do another incantation, something like what you did with the saltshaker?"

"I'm afraid it's not a bag of tricks," Astrid said. "You know, I'm sensitive sometimes to spirits? But, Alex, I don't feel anything here. Maybe because it's so old."

"Wouldn't you feel it?" he asked, searching. "In ghost stories a body that's been moved always feels wronged because it's not in its proper place."

Astrid shrugged. "Could be. But I'm not sensing it."

Alex backed up several yards from the circle, looking at the ruins as they cast their dark silhouettes against the gray sky.

He studied the grass, watching its dips and hills, thinking of the letter from Polidori. Something had to give them a stronger clue.

"The coarsest sensations of men," he said.

"Yeah," Astrid said.

"It's a line that brings us to this island because it was used in the part of the book that was set on this island. But that's not enough. You do the saltshaker magic and we get to this area, but that's not enough." He paused, thinking. "The coarsest sensations of men."

She put her hand on her hip and looked back at him, waiting for him to make a point.

Once again Alex wished he had Sangster with him. He shook his head. *Screw that. I can do this.* "What is a coarse sensation?"

Astrid went along with him. "Something . . . rough? Like rubbing a cat the wrong way?"

"Yeah . . ." Alex trailed off. "Everything here is rough. Rough Viking ruins, rough ancient Pictish ruins, rough Christian ruins. So maybe something else, maybe rough like, rough, like nasty."

"Vikings were pretty nasty," Astrid said.

Alex nodded. He'd read about some of the ways Vikings slaughtered their enemies. "But *sensation*," he went on. "That's like a feeling—a coarse sensation, right? But sensation, what else does that make you think of?"

Astrid thought. "Something amazing, or impressive, like a . . . spectacle?"

"A sensation is a *spectacle*." Alex nodded, circling again. "So what's a coarse sensation?"

"An ugly spectacle," Astrid said slowly. "A debased, big, ugly spectacle."

"Polidori lived here," Alex continued. "He had a hut here, which is gone now. But these ruins would have been here. He's telling us to look for the place of an ugly spectacle. There's only one thing I can think of that would fit that bill."

"Human sacrifice." Astrid's eyes lit up.

"You said that pain leaves a mark on the world, is that right?"

"Yes. Absolutely."

"Somewhere around here was a place of human sacrifice. Can you find that with your skills?"

Astrid nodded slowly. "I can try."

"Do you have to . . . cut yourself again?"

"I don't think so," she said, a little distant. "I just have to be willing to . . ."

"What?"

"Feel it."

Astrid stepped away from him a few paces, turning her back to him as she stood facing the sea. She bent and took off her shoes, and in her bare feet stood still in the grass, surrounded on all sides by the legacy of ancient peoples.

Alex thought he heard her whisper, *Mother Gretel, open me up, let me feel,* and then her whispers twisted into a language he couldn't understand.

The wind off the ocean bit his ears as it picked up, and he felt his flesh crawl, his mind tingling with something like the static. She was setting him off but in a different way. She began to tremble as she brought her open hands to her sides, and then her right arm shot out and up to her hair, and she pulled away a ribbon in one of her pigtails. The ribbon whipped in the wind and extended with her arm, flipping and pulling her hand off to her right.

He heard her let out a tiny sob and let go of the ribbon, and it drifted, landing in the grass.

Alex hesitated, and then Astrid started to walk toward the ribbon as it tumbled in the grass, finally catching in the crook of a stone.

The ribbon flitted against a long gray slab with a stone marker rising out of it. Alex walked swiftly toward it and dropped to the ground, staring at the carvings. Etched into the slab he saw a tall figure leading his followers. It was Pictish.

He was aware of Astrid dropping to her knees next to him, her hands in the grass. She wiped her cheeks. "Here," she said. "There were so many of them here. Pictish captives. They knew they were going to die."

"You can tell all that?"

"Only the feelings."

He put his hand on her shoulder. "I'm sorry you had to feel that."

"It's worth doing, Alex."

He nodded and pointed directly at the base of the slab. "Then we dig here."

He rose and scraped at the earth with his heel. "Let's churn up the earth around this wall."

Luckily the earth was soft, even a little muddy. For several minutes they scraped, kicking a few inches of earth.

Alex used the stock of his Polibow to rip away at the ground at the base of the stone. After a moment he saw a sliver of blue—another ribbon, rotten and disintegrating.

"*Yes*," he said. He began to dig around the ribbon, tearing away chunks of dirt at least a foot down, exposing the ribbon as he went and widening the hole.

He looked back, studying the space between the slab and the strips of stone in the earth nearby. Was there room for a casket, even a child's casket?

Finally the ribbon ended in a knot, and Alex felt past it, swiping earth aside to reveal an iron ring. He brushed more dirt aside, exposing old, mottled metal. Breathing harder now, he began to dig and run his fingers along the metal, finding edges that he desperately tried to clear. "It's a box," he said. "Help me with this."

They tugged at the iron ring and wrestled with the box in the earth, watching the dirt slide away. It wasn't a casket at all. It was a box about a foot long and seven inches wide.

With a great heave they wrenched it free, and Alex fell back, sprawling on the grass before catching himself and setting the old metal box on the grass. Then he rose and kneeled next to it, Astrid joining him.

"I don't know. You think we should take it back to the lighthouse and inspect it there?" Astrid asked.

"No way; I want in this thing." Alex clawed at a rusty clasp on the front of the box. It was not locked. "Okay, this could be . . . I don't know. It could be awful."

He breathed, flipped the clasp slowly, and pried the metal box open, forcing the ancient, rusted hinges. For a moment he hesitated, then looked at the contents. He saw a slim leather-bound booklet, held closed with a strand of leather, and a glass jar with a wide cork.

Alex picked up the jar first, holding it up. It was impossible to see through a layer of dust that had caked around it. Alex swiped at the dust and held it up again, and watched as strands of sunlight glinted off a swirling lock of human hair.

"That," said Alex, "is DNA."

"What about the rest?" Astrid said. She picked up the book, which seemed to be only a few pages long. She undid the string and opened it. Alex could see the writing was a dramatic, clear longhand, in English.

"*'On my greatest failure, a testament of John William Polidori. In 1822 . . . ,'*" she read aloud, and then fell silent. "This isn't right," she said, handing him the book. "He's your founder. You be the first to read it."

Alex's eyes shot across the page. He did not speak again until he had read it through.

CHAPTER 25

"All that is left of Allegra is this." Alex gestured at the jar with the book in his hands. The cold, damp wind lifted Astrid's hair as she listened, and he handed the book to her.

"Go ahead, read it," Alex said. "But the gist is this: In 1822, John Polidori, the doctor who had worked for Lord Byron and broken off with him after Byron began to show signs of vampirism, was supposed to be dead. By this time he had already gone underground and formed the first team that would be known as the Polidorium. But he moved much of his work here, because he was determined to save Byron's littlest victim, a victim Byron had not vampirized but had injured with neglect.

Byron's daughter, Allegra. Polidori bribed the nuns at the Italian convent where Allegra had been placed, where she was wasting away, and he took her himself.

"Even as he gathered information on vampires and the movements of Lord Byron, Polidori fled the country with the five-year-old Allegra, and brought her to a modest home he built here, on the Brough of Birsay. Here he wrote letters to his growing list of comrades and researched vampires, and watched over the girl as she grew, not for a year or two, but for over ten years. For ten years Polidori stayed right here, studying and working by correspondence.

"Right here," Alex said again, pointing at the meager foundation in the shadow of the Pictish stones, "was the nucleus of the entire vampire-hunting organization. And then in 1831, he made a mistake. That year, nine years after he had fled, Polidori returned to England to bargain with Mary Shelley, to convince her to put clues about Lord Byron's plans to rule the earth into the new introduction to her long-awaited new edition of *Frankenstein*. When he returned, he must have felt very satisfied. He and the now fifteen-year-old girl were living a happy life while he received letters from hunters around the world, and he sent clues as to the whereabouts of Lord Byron and the other vampires whom he would come to call clan lords."

Alex tried to envision this life as he spoke. Were there many visitors for him and Allegra beyond the mail that came infrequently? Local farmers in other huts, fisherman? Were they part of the community? The short testament did not say.

Astrid was reading, but Alex went on. "It took another year for the catastrophic result of his visit to Mary Shelley to occur. The Scholomance, which Byron had taken over, tracked Polidori back to the Brough of Birsay and dispatched a small force to take vengeance. They did not even touch Polidori, though he begged them to. What they did was worse: They took Allegra.

"After that, Polidori never forgave himself. He returned to Europe and redoubled his efforts. What I know from Sangster is that in the late 1800s he met Abraham Van Helsing and was able to prepare him for the attempted invasion of England by the clan lord Dracula. And Polidori did face Byron again, several times."

"And Allegra?"

"Never heard from," Alex said. "Who knows? Killed. Turned into a vampire, and then killed. But Polidori's greatest mistake was also his gift to the world: the clues he planted in *Frankenstein* to warn of Byron's return."

"I can't believe she was *alive* when she was here." Astrid was struggling with the same thing Alex was, that all this time they had been looking for a corpse, and it was a corpse that in all likelihood would never be found.

"Can you imagine? Polidori glosses over it, but imagine you've raised a child as your own, and then see her taken like that—and you know what's going to happen. If she isn't killed, she'll be perverted, poisoned, made to tear the flesh of humans, drink their blood. And you're powerless to stop it."

"It's horrible," Astrid agreed.

"Yeah, but you know what's even worse?" Alex continued. "Polidori did all this work while he knew that the vampires were watching him. He could have sent Allegra back to Claire, but he took it on *himself* to raise her. He put her at risk, even more than Byron had with his neglect. He was fixated on his work, the way all of his organization is still fixated on its work. And what's most disgusting of *all*—" He paused.

"What?"

"He left this." Alex held up the jar. "The one thing we need to stop Byron or Claire from using the Triumph of Death. Hair, DNA, from their loved one. Most likely he even picked this place to live because of the ley lines here, because he thought this would be the place for the Triumph to be set off, if it ever was. So there you are: He's overcome with grief, and he still thinks to leave us the hair."

Astrid put down the book. "You're being hard on him."

"Only because I know the type." Alex put the jar into his go package next to the vial gun. He heard them clank together. He felt weighed down by the jacket and the Polidorium, sullied by this work once again. He swallowed back an irrational welling of tears.

Astrid went to put her hand on Alex's shoulder, and he looked up at her, and if she was about to say something, it was interrupted when Alex gasped.

An enormous red claw was swinging as a nuckelavee rolled up behind her, striking Astrid and then Alex across the head. He saw the earth he had disturbed rising up to meet him.

When he awoke, the Brough of Birsay had been transformed into a world of ice and death.

CHAPTER 26

"Wake up, hon, or you'll miss it."

Woozily Alex felt his eyelids fluttering, and there was something caked in them. He realized he was seeing through mud and blood that had flowed down from his head wound. He blinked again, forcing his eyes open as though they were encrusted with sleep.

He felt numb, and cold, and didn't wait to feel anymore because Elle was standing in front of him, the black marks around her eyes, a brown hood pushed back to reveal her spiky blond hair.

Ask the questions.

What's going on?

I'm in a room, white, ice, ice all around. Elle is in

front of me and behind her I see sky. I see a wide window looking down on the island, and there's a platform with vampires on it. We're in an observation area, like a theater box seat. We seem to be in Antarctica—no. It's the Brough of Birsay, and it's covered in ice.

Where's Astrid? There, next to me—waking up. She's against the wall with a skull vampire watching her, and Elle is pacing, and Astrid's hands are . . . my own hands are numb, encased in ice.

What do you have?

"Hey!" Elle yelled, snapping her fingers in front of his face. "It's time. You get to watch."

"Watch what?" Alex asked wearily.

"Out there," Elle said, pacing on the ice floor, pointing out the viewing window. "The Triumph? It's about to begin."

Alex was watching past her, and even now he could see the platform where an even larger version of the satellite dishes in Bruegel's painting had been erected, with stairs leading up to it, and a pulpit. There were vampires milling about.

Everything ice. The island covered in it, this platform and box seat structure. "Icemaker did all this?"

"Yes, he did," Elle said. "Right here where the ley lines cross. I imagine the Queen would have done just fine on her own, but you gotta admit, Lord Byron lends a certain style to the proceedings."

Now Alex saw him, out the window and down below, about two hundred yards away—Icemaker himself, restored to his glory, his feeble leg replaced by an icy, thick hoof. He was waiting, like the rest of them.

"So you were right." Alex started moving his fingers, or trying to, but they were stuck. He didn't have much time or they would be frozen and lost, and he tried desperately to play it cool while he cursed at his blood, praying he could move it into his fingers. He was in a sweater, his jacket on the floor in the corner next to his go package and Astrid's bag. "She is a Queen, huh?"

"The greatest we're ever gonna have," Elle said, "a master of magic and of vampirism."

"Haven't we done this before?" Alex asked. "I don't get why you don't just kill me."

"Alex," Astrid said, trying to pull her own hands free, "don't tempt them."

"Oh, I'd love to," Elle said. "You know that. But Lord Byron has always known that the way to deal with the Polidorium is to make them suffer. You get to watch as your world plunges into darkness." She leaned in close. "So it's not up to me. But death does come next. And you won't be first."

"Make them suffer, the way Byron made Polidori suffer by stealing away his foster daughter?" Alex asked. He was moving his fingers, but not enough. The ice was curdled through the strands of his sweater cuffs and wouldn't allow him to move. *Keep working on it.*

Elle shrugged. "If you say so. I don't get caught up in ancient history."

He kept moving his fingers in the ice, feeling his blood begin to flow. "What are you gonna do when we're gone? I thought I'm basically your whole purpose for being right now. Aren't I your assignment?"

"Get over yourself, Al; I've had hundreds of assignments."

"And yet you'll never be a clan lord. Must be awful, at your age."

"Clan lord? What, you've been studying up? You don't know how we're organized. It takes longer than—"

"Well, I mean, shouldn't you want advancement? What was your first assignment? Watching someone like me, I'll bet. You strike me as basically a good, loyal follower, but not much more."

Elle was looking through the window and held up a hand. A small group of vampires, all in red robes, was approaching the platform, and among them the Queen, on horseback.

Alex watched her. "Why were you so upset about the empty coffin?"

"What?" Elle looked back at him. "The Queen wanted it intact."

"Oh, so you knew it would be empty."

"No . . ." Elle shook her head. "You want to know my next assignment? I have to find that damn corpse."

She doesn't know that Allegra was taken alive by the vampires. Alex laughed, then. "Good luck. It's dust."

"What did you say?"

"I said it's *dust*. Allegra Byron was taken by vampires. She probably *became* a vampire and was most likely killed a hundred years ago, probably by *my* people, and it was a dot on the register of vamps killed. The Queen will never get that daughter back, and you know what? They're *both* lucky that way."

"Taken by . . . *what*?" Elle seemed staggered by this, and Alex didn't waste too long staring at her face. Instead, he spat.

Elle cursed and wiped the spittle off her face, and as she did so, the other vampire came forward, putting a clawed hand on Alex's throat. "Settle down," the vampire ordered Alex.

Alex brought one leg up and kicked the second vampire in his knee. The vampire fell and smacked into the wall next to him. As Elle began to reach out, Alex twisted his leg again, pushing his weight on the vampire's neck. There was a heavy crack as the vampire's neck broke and he fell against Alex, shaking and disabled.

The vampire began to moan, and Elle was yelling, "Shut up!" as she looked out the window. Finally she went over to Alex's go package and drew out his Polibow. Alex prayed the bolt wouldn't go straight through the vampire, and it didn't when Elle shot; the bolt went in the vampire's back and he exploded.

Alex felt fire and heat push up around his sleeve and he yanked, feeling his skin scrape as he pulled his hands free of the ice.

"What's the matter, Elle, something not seem right?" he asked as he dove for his go package, feeling inside. He grabbed his dagger and rolled out of the way as she shot at him with the Polibow. "You wanted that body to be in that graveyard pretty desperately. Because when it wasn't you howled like a wounded animal. I think that's when you realized something you've been told wasn't true. I saw you, and when that casket flew open, something stopped being real for you." He had the go package slung over his shoulder and reached in, pulling out the jar. "But *this* is real, isn't it? This is her *hair*. This is the last of her human life, and I'll bet all memory of that has been ground right out of her."

"Shut up!"

"And you know what? If she didn't die, then Elle, I'm truly, truly sorry for what I'm going to have to do." Alex kicked the Polibow out of her hands as she shook her head, distracted. Elle was not herself now; she was troubled and had been since she had seen that coffin fly apart in the streets of London.

He fired it once and watched as the bolt sailed straight through Elle's shoulder, pinning her to the wall. She started twisting it, and Alex reached for Astrid's bag. He needed to get her hands free; he needed a spell to melt her bonds. She had said she had one. *Find the right spell. Find the right freaking jelly bean.* He emerged with one of the spell cartridges that Astrid had made and held it up. "This one?" he asked.

Astrid shook her head. "No!"

Elle tried to yank the bolt free, but her flesh was sizzling against it. "Don't move," Alex said to the vampire, "or the next one goes in your heart." He turned back to Astrid. "This one?"

Astrid nodded, and he ran over to her and held it near her hands. "*Fire*," she whispered, and as Alex pulled his hand away she turned her head, and the spell erupted, freeing her hands in a melting blur.

Alex ran to the window. The Queen was talking now,

at a dais in front of the satellite dish tower. She was raising her arms, chanting.

Alex gave the Polibow to Astrid. "Would you watch her?"

"I don't get it. Why don't we just—"

"Because we might need her." He was digging through his go package to find the vial gun. He brought it out, found one of the half-full vials, and then started to open the jar.

Suddenly Elle kicked out, smashing the Polibow out of Astrid's hands and screaming as she pried herself off the bolt.

Astrid screamed, forcing her hands to move as she bent down to rummage through her bag. She emerged with a six-inch green baton that she flicked, and it telescoped instantly into staff-length. She brought the staff to Elle's neck. "Now can we kill her?"

"No, we really might need her." Alex slid the lock of hair into one of the vials and clicked it into the vial gun. "We have to get closer."

They moved out of the box with Alex's Polibow firmly to Elle's back and into the open air. As they held Elle at the top of a stairway that ran down to the platform, Alex took a moment to admire the island, an eighth of a mile of ice and snow.

"It's a vampire wonderland," he said as Astrid forced

Elle down the stairs. They reached a plateau, behind a large crowd of vampires, who ignored them. The Queen was chanting still, her hands raised as she read from the text laid before her. The vampires were chanting in response, *Now is the time.*

Over the platform, from the satellite dish, darkness was spreading out and seemed to be pulsing in waves. Soon it would be done, and every street throughout the world would be madness.

"That's enough," Alex muttered as they drew close. Alex held up the vial gun, aiming for the Queen.

"It's not that easy," Elle hissed, spinning. Alex heard the Polibow go off, missing Elle, because Elle was a blur now, her arm swiping and smashing against Alex's, sending the vial gun flying.

All eyes turned, and a few of the vampires spotted them. Alex heard the chanting dissipate throughout the island.

He watched the vial gun with the sample of Allegra's hair and holy water clatter to the ice and slide against the platform where the Queen stood. It burst, spilling.

Icemaker turned then, registering mild surprise, and his first move was to throw a bolt of ice and bury the weapon.

Next he beckoned to Astrid and Alex, and Alex felt

Elle grab him by the shoulder and drag him forward, shoving him roughly until he was brought to them. He felt Astrid pushed next to him and they stood, defiant.

Elle forced Alex to his knees, and he was staring now at the feet of the unholy couple, the skeletal feet of the Queen and the icy hoof of Byron.

"My Lord." Elle bared her fangs. "It is time to be done with them."

"I love how you get all formal around him," Alex said. He was looking at the mound of ice where the weapon was buried. All that work by Polidori, all that work by some unseen force to lead them to the lock of hair, gone in a moment.

Oh, well. "It doesn't matter; I don't need it," Alex said. He had a dagger in his hand and a ball of holy water.

"Why's that?" Elle asked.

"Because whether you want to admit it or not, whether they ever saw fit to *tell* you or not, you are Allegra Byron," said Alex, suddenly rising and slicing at her forehead with the dagger. "And I'm taking some of your freakishly spiky hair."

A few strands fell into his hands, and as she was staring, dumbfounded, he slapped the strands of hair into his palm with the ball of water, and then smashed the glass ball against the heart of the Queen, feeling her rib cage crack as he pushed with all his might.

The Queen staggered, reaching out her hand to Elle, who was on the ground, trying to decide what to do. Icemaker was the first to regain his composure, and Alex felt a blast of cold slam into his chest and drive him back, sprawling across the ice, toppling handfuls of vampires. He heard Astrid, fighting already, and the Queen was screaming.

For a moment, Alex watched the Queen, Claire Clairmont, who had lived her whole life dedicated to finding power because what she had really wanted was to find a lost daughter, seem to grapple with all that she had learned in a few short moments. And then as she clutched at the holy water and the hair of the former Allegra Byron, she burst from the inside, and rained down on them all.

Elle ran toward the Queen, calling out, and flew to the blubbery, bony mass that remained of Claire. She threw herself at the feet of Lord Byron, her father.

"How much do you remember?" Alex yelled out. "Do you remember Polidori? There's no record of you before about sixteen, so do you remember that human life? Did you know that these were your parents? Because I'll tell you one thing." Alex pointed at Lord Byron. "*He* did."

And Byron, true to form, took one look at his child,

shot out a blast of ice, lifted off the platform, and fled into the winds.

Moments later, one of the vampires leaning over Alex exploded as Astrid's staff went through him, and Alex got to his feet. They stood back to back as the vampires surrounded them.

"Ooookay." Alex drove the silver-and-wooden dagger into the heart of one and turned, keeping his back to Astrid's. Far behind them, Elle was sobbing alone on the stage. Sociopaths or not, they could be felled by betrayal.

"Okay," Astrid echoed as she swiped with the staff, impaling a vampire. *Fwoosh* and *fwoosh* and *fwoosh*, and still they came. They were awash in a sea of skull-faced ghouls.

Not good. "I . . . ," Alex said, feeling her bony shoulders against his. A vampire nearly caught his hand and he yanked free. "Okay."

"Yep." She made a fireball and pushed through a bunch of them, and still they came.

Something whistled in the air, high and growing. Not far away there was an explosion of ice and holy water, with shimmering streaks of silver flying out, and Alex watched twenty of the vampires burst into flame and explode, setting off several more until the explosion dissipated.

"Alex," Astrid called.

The sound of rotor blades filled the air over his shoulder, and Alex turned with Astrid. Now he saw them, a streak of smoke as a missile emerged from the wing of a gunship helicopter. The missile struck the crowd, and Alex saw more vampires explode.

Four gunships, all told, and one of them swooped low. Alex saw the insignia of the Polidorium on the outside.

"Well, they could have been faster." Astrid fought on, but already the crowd was running for the ocean.

"Yeah, but I'll take it." Alex saw Armstrong, her leg still bandaged, and Sangster hanging out of the side of one of the gunships, firing away with machine guns. He watched all four mighty steel machines as they swooped like birds of prey, and the panicking, abandoned followers of the Queen began to run and die in disarray.

Alex and Astrid tore and shot and kicked as the gunships swept around them, scattering fire and ashes over the Brough of Birsay.

CHAPTER 27

The following morning, winter came to Lake Geneva with a sudden and unstopping sprinkling of snow, bringing an end to the strangest autumn of Alex Van Helsing's life. Alex was silent all during the ride with Sangster into the clearing in the woods and down into the recesses of the farmhouse.

Astrid had disappeared when they landed at the airstrip, off to the Orchard. He hadn't had the nerve to ask her when or if he would see her again.

It wasn't until Sangster had parked the van and they were walking through the hangar that he spoke.

"It eats you alive, doesn't it?" Alex said, stopping next to a Humvee, putting his hand on the hood just below a TALIA SUNT decal.

Sangster paused and looked back. "What?"

Alex was looking at the staircase that led up to the metal door, beyond which lay the secret world of the Polidorium. It was cold in the hangar and his words seemed to echo. For a moment he toyed with the clasp on his watch, which had a little silver cross, so that if he had no other weapons he could at least slap a vampire across the face and cause it pain. "There's nothing in the world I can imagine that is more horrible than vampirism, to see a person perverted and changed and made evil, and still have their brains and pieces of their personality."

"Yeah," Sangster agreed, but he seemed a little suspicious. "Yeah, that's fair. It's horrible."

"It was a trauma so great that Allegra Byron completely forgot her childhood when she became Elle."

"About that." Sangster looked genuinely puzzled. "How did you know that Elle was Allegra?"

Alex thought for a moment. "Actually, it was something that Ultravox said to me last month."

"Last month? You knew last month?" Sangster looked shocked.

"No, no," Alex said. "But Ultravox, when he wasn't busy telling his own lies, said something amazing that I remembered when Elle was at the graveyard in London. Ultravox told me that it takes *extraordinary* effort not to believe that which is of great comfort."

Sangster shook his head. "I'm not following you."

Alex said, "Elle was obsessed with reviving Claire. It was her personal mission to serve under the new Queen."

"That didn't make her the daughter, though," Sangster countered.

"No! In fact, when she went to the graveyard, Elle was completely thrown by the missing corpse of Allegra. She screamed like crazy, but she should have been thrilled. The weapon we were looking for wasn't there. After all, Allegra was Claire's daughter. Claire was going to gain power over the dead on the earth; she could find the body anytime. But Elle took it personally. She *needed* that body to be there," Alex said. "Because when it wasn't, Elle realized the truth."

"Allegra Byron," Sangster mused. "A little girl, extremely gifted and literate, a five-year-old who wrote letters to her father, begging him to come visit at the convent where he'd stuck her, utterly forgetting her mother."

"Allegra was dedicated to her father, and he neglected her," Alex said. "So then she's rescued by Dr. Polidori.

Snuck out of the country. Lives a quiet seaside cottage life in Scotland, until one day, the vampires come."

"And they turn her," Sangster said.

"Yes," Alex said. "At the age of sixteen, the vampires steal her away from Dr. Polidori. And who did those vampires work for?"

"Byron," Sangster said.

"Her father, who had ignored her, now a vampire, sends his minions to kidnap her and turn her into a vampire. So much trauma. A vicious death. The empathic centers of her brain fried. After ten years of a quiet life, she's then destroyed. I think there's no way she could consciously accept that Byron was her father then. And it's not like Byron took her in as a daughter. He denied her again, maybe never even saw or spoke to her. You know, if he had let her die, he might have stopped us from having a weapon against the Triumph. But of course he was too arrogant for that; he probably enjoyed denying her and keeping her alive. And she finally accepted that she was not Allegra. She had to."

Sangster shook his head again and let out a breath.

Alex continued. "Even though she disappeared, if I ever see her again I'm gonna ask her if Byron ever even spoke to her. But anyway: She became Elle, she served the Scholomance. She built up a story she could believe, that this was her life. Killing and maiming for a greater cause. But then Byron returns to all the vampires and tells the story of the Queen. And Elle wants beyond anything else to see this Queen."

Alex thought again of Ultravox's words. "What was of *great comfort* to Elle was to forget her childhood and remember only this vampire life, this mission, her place in the Scholomance, and now her service to the Queen. And of course it's a Queen who desperately wants to find her daughter. As tempting as it would have been to think of herself as Allegra, the truth about what happened to Allegra was too horrible to remember, even for her. And she guarded herself against the truth, the way everyone does."

Alex was picturing the coffin flying apart in the road. "It was the *coffin*. Elle needed to prove that everything she'd been told was true. That there was a dead little girl named Allegra who Claire would have gone back for if she could have found her. Elle wanted to prove to herself that her most awful, buried memories could not possibly be real. That the life she had built was real. And when the coffin shattered, so did her illusions about her life."

"But she held on," Sangster said. "You said at the Brough of Birsay she still kept on as usual."

"Nah, you should have seen her," Alex said. "She was losing it. She was fighting not to accept it all." He thought of Icemaker, lifting into the air with a snarl. "Because who would? In the end, he left again. And you know what's worse?"

"What?"

Alex sighed. "I took her mother away again."

Sangster said, "You can't think of it that way."

"Because they're sociopaths, right? It was still a cruel thing I did."

"I don't accept that," Sangster said. "It was a necessary thing. You didn't torture anyone. You didn't kidnap anyone. You killed a vampire to stop a terrible thing."

"Vampirism twists and distorts. But, Sangster, we twist and distort ourselves in response. John Polidori was willing to risk his only loved one—this adopted child—to fight vampires. And look at you."

Sangster had gotten quiet, but now he gave that half-smile of his. "What about me?"

"I mean, you can't get *away* from the Polidorium. And you know, between you and me, being an English teacher: not so bad."

"Why, thank you."

Alex nodded. "I know *one* person who walked away from this life, and that was my father. He quit. So what I want to know is: Is this my life now? I got bit and would have died if Hexen hadn't whisked me away. The doctor, Kristatos, she showed up at work one day and now she's dead—because of me. Is that a picture of my life; are these visions of my life?"

"Well, think of it this way," said Sangster. "If you hadn't been on the ball, the world would have ended in darkness. So maybe it *is* a picture of your life, and maybe that picture is also not so bad."

Alex shook his head. "I just feel . . . like there's always another door to go through. Like we're always being played. Someone went to the trouble to tamper with a painting that led us to Harrow, and finally to hidden DNA in *Scotland*."

"Blacktowers," Sangster said. "Well, we're gonna try to find out more about them."

"Oh, sure," Alex said. "And you know what, there will probably be a secret group behind them, too."

"Oh, for the love of—" said Sangster, running a hand through his hair. "Look, Alex . . ."

"And you know, I wanted to go to that formal last month, I mean, that's just an example."

"Oh, my God, you're killing me. Time out." Sangster jabbed his hands together. "Now you've done your monologue, so just hang on. First of all, I didn't stop you from going to the ball, the vampires did that, and you still made it, so give it a rest. But second of all, here's what I know."

Sangster put his hands on Alex's shoulders and hunched forward, like a coach talking through a football player's face guard.

"You. Are. Special. You're off the charts. We don't even have a word for what you can do. The Polidorium was founded by a doctor who wanted to save the world and who held his organization together with both hands until he died. You're not like that. You can sense evil. You have reflexes and adaptive ability that we can't even begin to understand. You inherited it from your mother, a witch, and your father, who passed you genes that go back to Abraham Van Helsing and farther back than that. Hexen, an organization that's so secretive that we wondered if they'd all been destroyed, came out of hiding for you. For *you!*"

Sangster let go, straightening up. He smoothed down his jacket and continued. "You know what I think? I think it's possible that this Blacktowers group has secrets for you, and if you want, we can try to learn those secrets. And I have a feeling you'll learn even more about yourself, but it'll still come down to the same thing: You. Are. Special." Sangster shook his head.

"I got bit, too," Sangster went on. "And I kept some of the curse and it makes me a little faster and a little quicker to heal. And it's nothing—*nothing* compared to you. Now, I'm not even gonna call you a whiner because I know better; I think you're a gentle and kind young man, and your questions are good. You can mourn not having a normal life. But don't for an instant regret the life you have. We don't need you," he said flatly. "The *world* needs you."

They stood there for a moment. Sangster patted Alex on the shoulder. "Come on, let's go give Carreras his debrief, tell 'em all how you saved the planet. And then you gotta get to class."

"Talk about a monologue," Alex said as they walked. "You should give speeches for a living."

"I'm a teacher; I already do."

"Too early for class, though," said Alex. It was seven in the morning. "I'm hoping to make it back by breakfast time."

"Great, see? You get to have a normal life," said Sangster as they hurried up the stairs.

CHAPTER 28

Paul, Sid, and Minhi didn't notice Alex at first when he wandered into the cafeteria and hung near the entrance. He took a moment to watch them, and saw that Sid was making them laugh with some extended story where he needed to pantomime being hung upside down. Minhi and Paul were holding hands, and Alex searched himself for the jealousy that so recently had tinged his soul whenever he saw them, and couldn't find it. For a moment he touched his neck, feeling the tenderness of the injury there, already almost healed.

Astrid came around beside him and leaned back against the door frame, holding a stack of books.

Alex turned toward her and smiled. "Astrid." He felt

his chest brim with something like shock and relief at once. "I thought you went back to the Orchard."

"You went back to the farmhouse," she said with a laugh. "We both have these places. We work there; we don't have to live there."

"Thank God for that," Alex said, watching her bright eyes shine. For a moment it was strange seeing her without an army of vampires trying to tear them both limb from limb. He wondered if her expandable staff was hidden in the pack she had slung over her shoulder. He found himself looking down and said, "I was afraid you weren't coming back." It sounded like a weak thing to say, but he said it just the same.

"Really?"

"Yeah, you know, weird stuff happens around here," Alex said. "Icemaker's still out there. And you never know when the chess team might suddenly all get cursed and turned into . . . giant . . . spiders. . . ."

"A giant spider curse?"

"Right, and I'm just guessing but I'm pretty sure we'd have to go to Egypt for that, and I hate to fly alone. Plus there's *Elle*—"

Astrid took his hand and patted it with her other hand. They both looked at each other and Astrid leaned over and kissed Alex on the cheek.

Alex smiled and looked down for a moment, then turned back to watch his friends, still clowning at breakfast.

"What are you looking at?" Astrid asked.

"I think I'm looking at the rest of my life," he said. Astrid threw a glance around the cafeteria and tilted her head, as if considering.

"For now," Alex clarified.

Astrid smiled, and together the pair walked to the breakfast table and began the day. There may well have been evil things watching, but for the moment they lay only in wait.

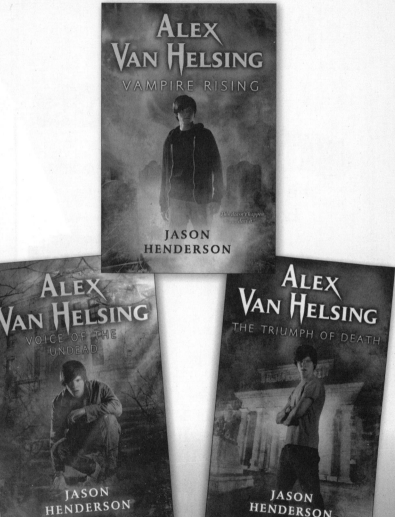